defying gravity

KENDRA C. HIGHLEY

Entangled Publishing, LLC
2614 South Timberline Road
Suite 109
Fort Collins, CO 80525
Visit our website at www.entangledpublishing.com.

Crush is an imprint of Entangled Publishing, LLC.

Edited by Heather Howland
Cover design by Heather Howland
Cover art from iStock

Manufactured in the United States of America

First Edition July 2016

For Mrs. Van Deman
who knew even Juniors in high school
need Story Time Fridays

and

Jean Shepherd
who made Story Time Fridays excellent

Chapter One

PARKER

"Where *is* she?"

Parker paced back and forth, his boots leaving tracks in the snow. He probably looked like a caged cougar, but he couldn't help it. "Doesn't Miller know there are trails to be shredded? In this lifetime?"

His brother, Luke, chuckled. "Zoey always makes us wait, bro. How about we make *her* wait this time?"

"No." Parker stopped to scan the entrance again. Still no sign. He knew she was in Aspen. Her plane had landed ninety minutes ago.

Great, now he was a caged cougar *and* a stalker.

Luke's sigh held an "aren't these kids cute?" note. "Oh, I forgot—Peanut Butter can't go without Jelly."

Parker shot him a look. "Can't you think of a more original nickname for me and Zoey?"

Luke shrugged. "Shoe fits...but if you're going to suggest something like Bert and Ernie or Leonard and Penny, I'm take points off."

"For what?" Parker asked.

"Because life isn't a sitcom, young apprentice. I'd be forced to charge you with a ten second penalty on our first run with Zoey." Luke shook his head, amused. "Not that I need the head start."

Parker's shoulders bunched up around his ears. *Young apprentice? Seriously?* "Are you really that eager to have your ass handed to you up on East Wall? Because if that's your deal, I don't need to wait for an audience."

"Ass handed to me? On a double black?" Luke laughed, and the crowd of girls lingering nearby giggled. He made a show of winking at them. "Since when? Last I checked, jibs were your thing, kid, not flying down a hill."

Parker went back to pacing, not bothering to answer. Luke had taught him how to board, but Parker had become the better shredder, both in speed and style. The student surpassing the master, or some Yoda shit like that. Not that his brother saw it. After winning tons of amateur downhill races, Luke still thought he was king of Snowmass. His horde of groupies thought the same thing, which made it hard for Luke to believe there might be someone a little better living in his own house.

"Seriously, we could hit a blue and be back before she shows." Luke nudged him off track. "Outrun me, and I'll let you borrow the Jeep whenever you want it."

Tempting offer—Luke's two-year-old Jeep was a much sweeter ride than Parker's ten-year-old Land Rover, a hand-me-down from their parents until he graduated—but not worth abandoning his post. "No deal."

"Aw, come on."

Parker shook his head firmly. "Nope. Go if you want, but I'm waiting."

"Fine, have it your way." Luke tromped off toward the

lifts, the group of girls trailing in his wake, hurrying to keep up.

Parker sighed. He loved that jackass—most of the time—but everything was a competition between them. It had only gotten worse since Luke left for college last fall. Part of him wished his brother had stayed back in Arizona for the holidays.

He kicked at a pile of snow. For Parker, Zoey's arrival on the mountain went down as one of the top five things he loved. The other four had a lot to do with her, too: her smile, the way she egged him on, how they always thought the same thing at the same time, and the way she fit into his life like she was there all the time. So he'd wait, and be happy about it. Like Christmas morning, some things were better because of the anticipation.

Parker checked his phone. No texts. No anything. So he went right on pacing.

He'd been this way for years, watching the door for any sign when he was younger, and later, prowling around Snowmass resort, hoping she'd hurry up. Sure, he had his own friends in Aspen, both at school and at Snowmass, but Zoey was the only person who'd known him before he could walk. Their parents had become best friends in college in Texas and even though his parents had moved to Colorado, the Millers kept in touch, going so far as buying the house next door as a vacation home. As far back as he could remember, Christmas and the month of July meant Zoey. She made the holidays what they were, every single year.

Would this be the year he told her how he felt? He'd vowed to do it over the summer, but never managed to get her alone. Luke had lurked around like his purpose in life was to chaperon the "kids." His brother couldn't resist being center of attention, and what better way than showing up his "little" brother for Zoey's amusement?

Parker grumbled to himself. *This year* he'd find a way

to ditch Luke long enough to tell her. Zoey going from best friend to crush two years ago had been a strange and wonderful thing…and falling in love with her last Christmas break had been even more overwhelming. He knew it was a risk to their friendship. A big one.

Some things were worth the risk.

The crowd at the entrance started doing strange things. For one, it parted like the sea before Moses. For another, guys stopped dead in their tracks…and those who didn't stop ran into walls or tripped over their own feet. The women and girls around these guys started rolling their eyes, some good-natured, some not so much.

Parker's heart hammered like a drunk carpenter had taken over his pulse.

Zoey was on the mountain.

She breezed through the crowd in a lime-green ski suit, her snowboard resting against her shoulder. Blond hair streamed out behind her under the hot pink knit cap she'd been wearing since they were kids, and her cheeks were flushed with the cold. Her smile could stop traffic…no, really, it *had* stopped traffic. The sudden loss of coordination among the men near the entrance was proof.

He could only imagine what her *real* smile—the one she only gave him—could do.

Wait. No. He didn't want her smiling at any other guys that way.

She searched the crowd, oblivious as always to the way people stared, and Parker waved. Laughing, she barreled straight at him, tossing her snowboard to the side, before knocking him into a snow drift. They landed in a clatter of boots, boards, and limbs, with her on top.

Her grin lit up the world. "Parker Madison! How the hell are you?"

His entire body went supernova hot. He could feel every

inch of her, despite the layers of ski clothes separating them. *Jesus.* He choked back a groan and tried to think of anything other than how perfectly they fit together. If she felt how his body responded to her…

No, not happening.

He sighed heavily and brushed melting snow from her cheek. "How am I? Well, Miller, I'm bored." *Lie. So much lying. Whole mountains of lie.*

"Bored?" She blinked at him. "I'm not *that* late."

He pretended to scowl at her, enjoying the close-up look at her baby-blues. Huh, was she wearing *mascara?* Since when did she wear makeup on the mountain? Not that he was complaining—she looked amazing. "Zoey, two ages of the universe passed by while I've been waiting for you. Maybe even three."

"Is that so?" She smiled again and tugged on his cap. "I missed you."

There's the smile he'd been waiting for. His mouth went dry and he had to swallow a few times before he could speak. Maybe he should just kiss her instead. "Yeah?"

"Yeah." She clambered to her feet, then gave him a hand up. "Speaking of missing people, where's Luke?"

Of *course* she'd ask about his brother. Damn it. "He left without us."

"Figures." Lucky for his brother, she didn't sound the least bit annoyed. "I think we should leave *him* behind. Want to take me down a blue so I can get my legs back in shape?"

"I guess so," he said with a dramatic droop to his shoulders, waving toward the lifts. "I *was* planning to show off for you some, but we'll take it easy today."

"Showing off. Some things never change, do they, Madison?" She bumped him with her hip, and a rush of heat ran down his side. "Fine. You can show off on a blue just as easily. How about Creekside?"

They walked to the lifts in silence, bumping shoulders every few steps. With most girls, this would be awkward, but Zoey knew what he was thinking before he did, most of the time, so their silences were full and complete. She paused to tuck some hair behind her ear, and he blinked, realizing what was different. She had actually done her hair, and she *was* wearing makeup. This wasn't how Zoey usually rolled. He thought she looked great in pajama bottoms, a sweatshirt, and her hair up and messy, but she'd gone all out today, and it got his attention.

She glanced at him. "Okay, Mr. McStaring Pants, what's with the look over? You're giving me a complex."

She was smiling, but Parker's cheeks flushed at her catching him. He laughed it off. "I just noticed you look different than normal, is all. Where's the ponytail? You never wear your hair down. Did you agree to pose in one of those cheesy resort brochures or something?"

She shrugged, although it looked like her cheeks grew a little pinker, too. "I thought I'd make an effort for once, is all."

For him…maybe?

"Besides, I couldn't go to the airport looking like a mess."

Or not. Parker frowned. "Why? Were you scared the TSA wouldn't approve?"

Zoey looked away. "Something like that."

Something in her tone told him she wasn't being honest, but he knew enough to let it go. Sometimes Zoey needed space to breathe, and he liked being the guy she could count on to make that happen. "That's cool. No big deal."

They made it to the lifts, and the line for the quad wasn't short, but when was it? He didn't mind the wait, not with Zoey by his side. Guys were staring at him in envy, and he straightened his shoulders. "How was the trip here?"

"Fine. The cold was a shock—it's sixty-five in Dallas today."

"That's spring weather. I'd be outside in shorts." He shook his head. "How do you even stand it out here, southern girl?"

She gestured at the mountain rising about them. "I accept it as a part of this. Without the cold, I wouldn't have snow to shred." She nudged him in the shoulder. "Or winter break with you. I live for this, you know."

She was going to kill him. He swallowed. "Yep. It's definitely worth it."

"Uh huh. All you heard in that sentence was 'Or winter break with you,' wasn't it?" She threaded her arm through his and leaned her head on his shoulder.

Yep, he was going to fall over dead. He tucked her head under his jaw. "That *is* the most important part."

She laughed a little. "I do like the snow a lot, though… it's a tossup."

"Arrow, straight to the heart." He spun her out and twirled her around. "Guess my ego needed that."

"You know I love you." She gave him a quick hug, probably not realizing how bad that stung, because it wasn't the "I love you" he wanted to hear.

"Love you, too," he murmured into her hair before reluctantly letting her go.

The line shortened, and they took their places next to an older couple. The quad chair swung up, catching them behind the knees. Zoey plopped into her seat off-balance with an, "Oof!" then laughed. "People at school would never believe I'm a total spaz in real life."

In real life—because she didn't see her time at home as genuine. It made him sad. "You aren't a spaz."

"No?" Her expression turned a little wistful. "In some ways I wish I could be, though. At least every once in a while."

He wound an arm around her. "People would love the real you just as much, you know. Maybe more."

She rested her head on his shoulder. "Maybe. Back there

I'm Class President Barbie, the girl with all her shit together and no doubts about who she is, or what she wants. You're the only person I can trust with *me*."

It made him a selfish bastard, but he loved that she felt that way—that she could be herself with him, and only him. Doubts and all. "Would it make you feel better if I tripped over some stuff, too?" He gave her a little smirk. "I could even fall when we get off the chair at the top, even things out a bit."

She smacked his chest. "You know what I mean. You don't care what I look like or what I do. That makes you a rare beast, Madison."

"Mmm. 'Rare beast.' I like that. Maybe I'll get that tattooed on my—"

"Yeah...no. Do *not* even go there." She straightened and took a deep breath. "Just look at that view. This is what I've been waiting five months to see."

He took a deep breath, too, enjoying the bite and tang of pine in the air. The ski runs spread out below them, dots of color moving down the hill as people skied or boarded. The dark green tree boughs covering the mountains were speckled with white, glistening in the weak winter sun. Zoey was staring at everything, craning her head back and forth like she had to see it all, right this minute.

"The mountain will still be here tomorrow," he said.

"But it won't be the first look." She flashed him her quicksilver smile, then pointed down. "Is that Luke?"

Parker followed the angle of her finger. A guy in a red ski jacket was making one hell of a run down the hill, zigzagging through slower skiers and boarders, his cuts clean and precise. "Definitely Luke."

"Think he'll wait for us at the bottom?" she asked.

And miss a chance to show off for the kids? Never. "Yeah, he'll wait once he notices I'm gone. He knows I wouldn't leave unless you were with me."

"He still calling us PB&J?"

"Always."

"That doesn't bother me, you know, being part of our sandwich." She leaned against him. "I don't know how I got so lucky. My besties are the best."

The plural made him think to ask, because it made her happy when he remembered details about her life in Dallas. "And how is Paige?"

"She has a boyfriend! He's this adorkable math geek who would walk on fiery coals for her, all while solving a calculus problem in his head. As she deserves." Zoey looked up at Parker. "You deserve that, too."

He raised an eyebrow. "An adorkable math geek?"

She laughed. "No—someone who would walk on coals for you."

This was it. She'd totally given him the opening. Now all he had to do was say, "*How about you? And while we're at it, have any hot coals you need me to walk over? I might have to skip the math, but I could recite a poem instead,*" and she'd stare at him in confusion, then delight as she realized...

"Kids, our stop is coming up," the older man said. "Just thought I'd let you two lovebirds know, in case you missed it."

He said it kindly, but Zoey turned bright red. "Oh...no. We're friends, that's all."

With that, she hopped off the lift, leaving Parker to follow her. The old man gave him a sympathetic pat. "Sorry, kid. Maybe she'll come around."

Funny how obvious his feelings were to anyone but her. "Let's hope."

Chapter Two

ZOEY

Zoey's cheeks steamed in the cold, more from embarrassment than the chill. Lovebirds? What was that guy thinking, calling them lovebirds? Sure, Parker was cute and sweet and pretty much everything she'd want in a guy, but he was her *best friend*.

Lovebirds. Pshaw.

Why wouldn't her cheeks cool down? Parker had her back, utterly, completely, no doubt. He was the constant in her life. Her fixed point, her conspirator, her North Star. She couldn't imagine being as open, as brutally honest, as she'd been with him with anyone else. You don't risk a friendship like that, not ever.

Luke, though… She'd like to get closer to him—assuming she managed to catch his attention long enough for him to see how she felt about him. She'd probably have to take a freaking number, what with all the snow bunnies following him around Snowmass.

Zoey sighed, heart aching a little. While she was always glad to see Parker, she needed this trip to figure out if Luke could maybe feel something for a girl he'd watched grow up. She wasn't a kid anymore, not a tagalong or too young to do all the things he wanted to do. She was his equal—strong-willed and able to take on anything he could dish out.

But would he notice?

Luke would be at the bottom waiting for them...for *her*. And she'd made sure she was ready—though she hadn't counted on having to ride down the mountain before he saw her. Most of her hard work would disappear once they hit the run. Was mascara wind-resistant? Her hair certainly wasn't.

Ugh. This was so not the first impression she'd hoped to make this winter. When they'd left Aspen last summer, Luke had made a point to squeeze her arm and look right at her with his striking hazel eyes—green and brown and gold—and say, "I can't wait to see you again."

And people wondered why she didn't bother with dating guys at Alderwood. If they met Luke, they'd know.

"You coming?" she called back to Parker from the edge of the run.

"You waiting for an audience?" He skated toward her, then bent to fasten his back binding.

"No, I'm waiting for backup in case I have a total yard sale down there."

He smiled and joined her at the edge. He had a great smile, one she loved to see. The kind that told her she was important to him. "You aren't that rusty. I'm sure you'll keep your gloves and hat when you fall."

"As if." She sniffed. "I won't fall."

He slid back and forth. "Then what are we waiting for, Miller?"

He barely got the words out before she flung herself over the side. Chuckling, he launched after her, passing her, then taking languid cuts that put him behind her. It never failed to amaze her just how spectacular the Madison boys were on the snow. All the locals knew who they were. A fixture on Snowmass—handsome, athletic, talented. The guys every girl wanted, and every snowboarder watched.

Zoey wasn't a total slouch herself, despite the lack of practice time. The snow crunched in a satisfying way as she streaked down the hill. She'd been worried about her leg-strength—she'd taken it easy on the jogging after spraining an ankle last month—but it was like she'd never left Aspen. Her balance was spot on, and she took nice, clean turns as she made her way down Creekside trail. Something unwound inside her chest, a loosening of tension that always unspooled when her feet touched ground in Colorado.

It was a good feeling, but it nagged her nonetheless. Why didn't she feel this comfortable in her own skin at home? At home, her armor was flat-ironed hair and perfect makeup, great clothes and new shoes. She loved to dress up, but doing it every day, day in and day out, was wearing her down. Why was showing—even *being*—herself so hard?

She rolled her eyes. Because her place in the pecking order had been sealed in eighth grade when her bra filled out and her legs grew long. After that transformation, changing her look would've sent a wave of gossip from one end of Alderwood to the other. People would assume she was depressed if she showed up in leggings, a baggy shirt, and no makeup.

What would any of those poseurs think if they saw her now, streaking down the mountain like some kind of skater-culture fangirl? Or if they saw her pretend to talk in an Aussie accent for an entire day, just to confuse people when they asked where she lived? "Texas, mate!" tended to make people give her the eye, and Parker laughed every single time.

She neared the bottom, which was more thickly populated

with skiers and boarders, so she pulled her head out of the clouds and searched for tall, dark, and handsome in a red ski jacket.

She slid to a stop and took off her board. Luke had to be around there somewhere. Surely he hadn't taken off again, not when he hadn't even stuck around to say hi in the first place. Being with Parker had relieved that sting, but now she was impatient. She got up on her tiptoes to look over the heads of the crowd, but not even the fact she was fairly tall helped. It was like Aspen shipped in six-foot-plus tall men in special for scenery.

"Find him yet?" Parker asked, coming to a stop next to her. His slightly shaggy hair was windblown under his helmet and his cheeks were red, but he looked so alive. She wanted to feel as alive as he looked. When was her confidence going to kick in? She'd done her hair—and even worn makeup, which she never did up here—to impress Luke, knowing he liked put-together girls. She thought having her armor in place would help her nerves, but her stomach swooped at the thought of him checking her out.

She clasped her hands together to keep them from trembling. "No. Think he ditched us?"

Snow skidded in a trail behind her, a little bit nipping at her cheek. She whipped around, and there Luke was in all his dashing glory. Grinning, he said, "I didn't ditch you. I saw you on the lift, talked my way toward the front of the line, and came down after you, but you had a head start." Luke's smile made all kinds of promises and Zoey's chest prickled with heat. "So how's my best girl?"

She stepped into his arms gratefully for a hug, hoping she wasn't hanging on too long. Parker laughed like it was the funniest thing he'd heard. "Best girl. For how long? Today?"

Luke let her go and slid down to Parker, giving him a "shut up, little bro" look. Standing together, there was no doubt they were brothers: same dark brown hair, same hazel eyes, same nose, but that's where the similarities ended. Luke was six feet tall and compact, with the well-defined muscle, sharp jaw, and predatory gaze of a lady-killer. Everything he did was with economy of motion. Zoey defined it as "cat-like poetry" in her head, knowing full well Paige would fall over laughing at the very idea.

Parker, on the other hand, was taller than his brother, and long and lean, with slightly softer features and an open, friendly face. Quiet, sensitive, but no pushover, mothers around the world would sell the family silver for a chance at nabbing him for their daughters. Both Madison boys were smart, but one was direct and hardheaded, and the other was good-humored and artistic. Park would make a girl really happy someday.

Maybe as happy as she and Luke could—*would*—be.

"Guys, please don't argue." She gave them both an exasperated look. "It's my vacation, and I want to be happy. Everyone behaves when I'm around, remember?"

Both of them deflated a little. "Okay," they said in unison, then cracked up.

"Only Zoey," Luke said, "could say that to us with a straight face and expect us to listen."

Parker nodded. "Only Zoey."

Now everything was right with her world, having one Madison on her right, and the other on her left. "Who's taking me to Two Creeks for coffee?"

"After only one run?" Luke's tone was slightly teasing, but something a little more dangerous lurked underneath. "Surely you're up for something more exciting?"

She shivered inside her ski gear, doubting it was due to cold. "Maybe."

Parker was looking back and forth between them, a tiny line creased between his eyebrows. "Not a black diamond on day one. It's too much."

Luke shrugged. "I'm up for it."

"And you grew up on this mountain, asshat." Parker scowled at Luke. "She just got here. Let her take it easy today, and tomorrow we'll head up to the Headwall for a real run."

"Stop being so overprotective," Luke drawled. "She's not made of porcelain."

Zoey rolled her eyes and stepped between them. "*She* is right here, and capable of making her own decisions, thank you very much." She turned to Luke and smiled. "I appreciate the vote of confidence, but maybe a black is too ambitious for today." As much as she wanted to rise to the occasion, her ankle had started to hurt, and she worried the boys would have to carry her back down if it gave out on her. "You two can show off tomorrow."

"Show off, huh?" Luke gave her a lazy smile. "What are you hoping to see?"

She widened her eyes in pretend innocence, hiding how much that smile undid her. "How your new board handles."

It was a gamble, she knew it, but Luke loved showing off his skills. Parker was a better boarder than he let on, and maybe this would soothe his ego some, too. The Madison boys loved nothing more than trying to one-up each other. Didn't matter what: boarding, basketball in the driveway, darts, SAT scores, who could hit the trash can with a wadded up napkin from the farthest away—everything was a contest between them. She didn't like encouraging it, but sometimes setting up rules made them back off a little bit.

"Deal." Luke punched Parker in the arm. "How about it?"

"Yeah, okay." Parker didn't sound too happy about it, but at least he agreed to come. "Let's hit some more blues, then coffee's on me."

"Have I told you I love you today?" Zoey said, leading

them to the lifts. "Because Parker, I truly, madly, deeply do."

"Uh, yeah, you did tell me." Parker sounded suspicious. "You aren't going to order one of those crazy-expensive lattes, are you?"

"Mayyyybe." She grinned at him over her shoulder, making sure to catch Luke in the crossfire.

He winked back at her. "You have him wrapped around your little finger, don't you?"

"It's mutual, and you know it. Peanut Butter and Jelly, as you like to say." She linked arms with Parker. "Let's go have some fun."

And if she could manage to "accidentally" brush into Luke at some point, all the better. Because, as of right now, her plan to land Luke was progressing nicely.

She just needed to make sure she succeeded before he went back to Arizona.

Chapter Three

The crowd near Two Creeks was thinning out by the time they came down the hill one last time. The sky was fading to dusk, and the mountain threw shadows in strange designs on the snow. What would he give to create a ski resort like this? He could only hope his drawings were good enough to get him admitted to the Architecture college at Colorado State. He wanted to design it all, from ski huts to chalets to big resort hotels.

"What'cha doing?" Zoey called.

Parker realized he'd stopped to stare at the design of the café and the flow of traffic around it. "Just looking at buildings."

"Thought so. You had that analytical look on your face." Zoey was pink-cheeked and grinning, already looking more at ease. She'd also found time to put on more lip gloss, and he wanted nothing more than to figure out if it was flavored or not. *That* was a science experiment he'd volunteer for. First hand raised.

He swallowed a sigh. What would she think if she found out how much he thought about her? Probably tease him mercilessly. Still, he wished she could live here full time. Not just so they'd be together all the time, but because he thought she'd live a more chill life in Aspen. He hated how stressed out her school back home made her. She deserved to live in a place that made her feel complete, not pulled a thousand directions.

"So, Luke…" Zoey slowed to force Parker to wait on his brother. "How's life?"

Luke laughed. "That's a pretty broad question, Z. Care to narrow it down?"

She bit her lip and giggled.

Parker frowned. She…*giggled*? Zoey didn't giggle.

"Okay. Any girls we need to know about?" She tossed her blond hair over one shoulder, and her ears turned pink.

What the hell?

Luke bumped his shoulder against hers. "Not at the moment. Why, you know some?"

Zoey giggled again and playfully smacked his arm.

Parker's eyebrows knit together. Okay, this wasn't right. Why was she flirting with Luke? Did she like him? And what the hell was his brother doing flirting back? He needed to figure out what was going on before he made a colossal jackass of himself, confessing feelings she might never return.

The thought was pretty miserable, but pessimism wasn't his thing.

They dropped off their boards and tromped into the café. It was full of adult skiers having martinis and glasses of wine, but the baristas were still working overtime at their espresso machines behind the bar. Zoey would have her fancy latte even if he had to help make it.

After ordering—with Zoey asking for a quad grande

vanilla cinnamon soy latte, a phrase that made Parker's eyes cross and Luke laugh outright—they went to one of the round wooden tables in the corner of the café. Snow blew against the windows, but inside it was warm and quiet. Parker relaxed his shoulders and neck. Maybe he'd imagined the flirting. What if he hadn't, though? Would that change anything?

Watching her sip her ridiculous coffee with unabashed pleasure, he wasn't sure it would. So what if Luke picked up girls faster than a black sweater picked up lint? Zoey hadn't flirted with him before, at least as far as Parker knew. They weren't even particularly close, with Luke wandering off with his friends most of the time. Maybe she was being goofy. She had a habit of that—one of her more endearing qualities. It wasn't every day you found a model-gorgeous girl willing to wear the world's ugliest Christmas sweater or intentionally cross her eyes at ski patrol.

But…what if she *wasn't* being goofy? What if she really was flirting with his brother?

His stomach clenched and he sat up taller. *No.* He wouldn't let that stop him. He'd promised himself that he'd tell her how he felt, and he would.

It might be a little harder now, was all.

Zoey licked a stray bit of foam off her bottom lip. "What's the plan for tonight?"

Luke's eyes followed the move, and Parker wondered if he'd be arrested for putting his brother through the window. Ignoring Luke's obvious leer, he said, "Your family is coming over for dinner. We could do a movie or something after?"

"Works for me." She smiled brightly at Luke. "Sound good?"

He shrugged. "I might have plans. We'll see."

Zoey's smile faded, then returned, but it had a forced quality to it. "It's my first night in Aspen. You have a moral obligation to hang out with me."

"Us," Parker said firmly. "You have a moral obligation to hang out with *both* of us."

Luke's gaze shifted to him. "Really? Because I thought PB&J were fine on their own."

There was a challenge in those words somewhere. Fine, if that's how he wanted to play it, then Parker could, too. "We wouldn't want to ruin your plans. I can keep Zoey entertained all by myself."

Zoey choked on her drink. "C-can you n-now?"

He leveled a lazy smile her way—Luke wasn't the only one with that particular superpower. "Pretty sure I can, if you'd give me a chance."

Confusion flitted across her features. "Must be one hell of a movie we're watching."

Luke cleared his throat, bemused. "Mom said we're eating at seven. We better go home."

"Give me a lift?" Zoey asked. "I came on the tram because Dad wanted the car."

"They really should rent you a car of your own while you're here," Luke said. "Then Parker wouldn't try to steal my Jeep."

"For the next week I think the term is 'our Jeep,' asshat. Last time I checked, Dad was still making the payments on that beast." Parker held the door open for Zoey. "And I put gas in it, so what's the problem?"

"It's *my* Jeep. That's the problem."

Zoey groaned. "You two aren't going to argue for the whole week are you?"

If Luke was going to toy with Zoey all week, they damn sure were going to argue. Luke smirked at him, almost like he knew what Parker was thinking. Parker took one, deliberate step towards him.

Throwing up her hands, Zoey snatched the keys dangling from Luke's fingers. "I guess that's a yes. Look, I'm cold. I'll be in the car when you're ready to go."

"That girl." Luke shook his head as Zoey stalked over to the Jeep and let herself in—intentionally climbing into the driver's seat. "She's got our number, huh?"

"Yep."

"I like strong-willed girls—they're hot. Which complicates things."

"How?" Parker noticed a growl creeping into his voice. This wasn't going anywhere good.

"I think she has a thing for me." He shot Parker a slightly smug look. "Weird, huh? She's like a little sister, then, boom, suddenly she's not."

Parker stiffened. "She's still like a little sister to you."

Luke scoffed. "Oh, come on. You can't tell me you don't notice how gorgeous she is. She's not that pigtailed girl we grew up with." He let out an appreciative sigh. "I wonder if I should do something about her little crush."

Parker's hands fisted inside his gloves. Luke made dating Zoey sound like an amusing side-hobby. "I think you should leave well enough alone."

Luke shrugged. He *shrugged*. "I didn't say I *would* do something. It was a hypothetical. Why are you so pissy? Worried I'll break up your little sandwich?"

Parker turned and stalked for the car. "I'm worried you'll break her heart."

Chapter Four

ZOEY

Luke's Jeep smelled just like him: pine, wool, and a touch of danger. Okay, so maybe the "danger" was the faint smell of gasoline, but still. Zoey breathed in deep. This car said a lot about its owner. The red, four-door Wrangler was rugged but stylish, with its leather seats and manual transmission. It told her that the owner liked to stay in control, but wanted to look good doing it.

She giggled. Good God, when would she stop doing that? She sounded like a seven-year-old. She didn't like acting like one of his groupies, but she couldn't help melting a little every time he set eyes on her. And that sexy, lazy grin? Her bones turned to Jell-O.

Speaking of which—when had *Parker* mastered that skill? He'd flashed her a nearly identical, albeit slight more genuine, lazy grin when they were having coffee. Had he always done that and she hadn't noticed? Huh.

She glanced at the brothers standing just outside the

coffee shop, worried by the tension in the way they stood, facing off, having what looked like a semi-serious discussion out in the cold. They never discussed anything seriously. Ever.

Fought, yes. Discussed, no.

When they were younger, Luke and Parker fought all the time, giving her a chance to see what it was like to have brothers. She loved it—fights and all—so much that she was always lonely the first few weeks after coming home from Aspen. But this seemed different. Worse. Their postures were more dominant and wound-up, like Luke had pushed Parker one button too far.

She revved the engine to get their attention. Whatever was bothering them needed to take a rest. She didn't want to have to be their referee this trip. She'd done that three years ago when Luke "borrowed" Parker's board because his was broken…then broke Parker's, too. Parker, in turn, had thrown Luke's trophy from his first win at the Boardercross race into a snowdrift in the backyard and refused to tell Luke where he hid it. They didn't speak to each other for two-thirds of the vacation, leaving Zoey to organize all the activities and separate them when they made eye contact and fists started clenching.

Revving the engine did the trick. They both jumped slightly and turned to face the Jeep at the same time. Totally brothers, even if they were annoyed with each other. They started for the car. Parker stalked, barely hiding the fact that he was still really, really mad, but Luke swaggered behind him, like he'd hit his brother where it hurt, just as she'd suspected.

Seriously, what was wrong with these two?

Luke rapped on her window, flashing her a hundred-watt smile. "You can ride shotgun, but I'm driving, Sweet Cheeks."

Parker made a gagging sound. "*Sweet cheeks?* Miller, are you going to stand for that?"

Two pairs of hazel eyes focused on her, like the answer to

that question was the most important thing in the universe. What the hell was going on? "I'll let it slide this time."

She hopped out of the driver's seat and managed to brush her arm against Luke's chest as she passed by. Parker rolled his eyes and followed her passenger side. Once Luke's door slammed, she grabbed Parker's sleeve. "Is everything okay with you two?"

He shot Luke an unreadable glance. "Fine. I just need to talk to my brother about…boundaries."

Boundaries? Had he noticed her flirting with Luke, and Luke flirting back? Because that's what it had felt like—him flirting back. Was Parker mad because he thought Luke was messing with her? "I hope everything's okay now."

"It is what it is," was his cryptic answer, before he opened the front passenger door for her and shut it after she climbed in.

The Jeep's interior was so thick with tension on the ride home, Zoey couldn't bring herself to talk. That didn't stop Luke, though. "So, Zoey, there's a great new club downtown. Eighteen to enter. How's a night out dancing sound?"

Parker jumped in before she could answer. "Sounds good to me. How about it, want to join us?"

Luke's jaw tightened, and Parker looked pleased with himself. Oh, great. She'd been right. Parker didn't approve of Luke showing her that kind of attention. Sweet of him to be so protective, but she could handle herself. Still, the guys seemed strung out and she had to keep the peace somehow. She'd roll with Parker as a chaperone for now, but try to find a way to get Luke alone so she could gauge how he felt. "Sounds fun. I brought some going-out clothes just in case. When?"

Please say tonight. Please ditch your bros and let me show off my red dress. She thought about fluttering her eyelashes, but that was going too far. Or was it? Hadn't Paige's boyfriend, Ben, said something about her being a danger to others when she vamped it up? How much was too much?

Luke winked. "I'm booked tonight, and the club's closed Sunday through Tuesday, so we'll go Wednesday night. I overheard Mom say the parents are having an *Apples to Apples* tournament then, so it'll be a good idea to escape."

"God, I hope we never get that boring when we're old," she said.

Parker chuckled in the backseat. "Miller, when we're old, we're going to be smoking the youngsters up on the Cirque. They'll all be like, 'look at those geezers cutting a trail!' It'll be awesome."

She looked over the headrest to grin at him. "Then we'll put on our bifocals and get into our Caddie and drive home ten miles under the speed limit."

The skin around Luke's eyes tightened. "And what will I be doing?"

Wound up. Both of them. "You'll be with us, of course."

"The three amigos." Luke snorted. "Z, you know Parker and I aren't a package deal. Eventually we'll go our separate ways, and you've always stuck with Peanut Butter."

She shrank down in her seat feeling like she'd been sucker punched. "I'd hoped we could all still get together, like our parents do."

Hopefully, you and me with our kids, and Parker with his family. Wouldn't that be perfect?

"We will," Parker said, and Zoey caught him glaring at Luke in the rearview mirror. "We're friends forever, Miller. Luke doesn't stick to stuff, but I do, and I promise, I'll be there."

Luke's hands gripped the wheel so hard his knuckles turned pale in the dim light. "I'm not as temporary as you seem to think, *bro*."

Holy crap. Zoey waved her hands. "Okay, okay, stop. I don't know what the problem is, but you two either need to tell me or get over it. I can't referee if I don't know what I'm dealing with."

"It's nothing," Luke growled to the windshield.

"Nothing," Parker said.

Yeah, right. Because "nothing" had them in a really pissy mood.

Luke turned down their street. Lights were on in both houses—Zoey's a rustic two-story, and the boys' column-fronted colonial. Or so Parker told her—she wouldn't know the difference. Their windows gleamed a soft gold against the snow, welcoming them home.

"See you at seven," Parker called as she hopped out into the slush at the edge of the driveway.

She nodded, then half-skated up the frozen sidewalk to the front door. While Parker and Luke lived here year-round, her place was their second home. Her parents paid Parker to mow the lawn in the summer and bring in the mail, but it still felt lonely and stale the first day or two after they arrived. "I'm home!"

"Okay!" Dad called, probably in the kitchen. "Have fun?"

Had she? Interesting question. "Yeah, but the guys were kind of snarling at each other."

He came into the entry, drying his hands on a dishtowel, and gave her a quick side-hug. "You expected peace?"

"Not exactly." She chewed on a strand of her hair—a habit she was *very* careful to hide from her friends back home. "But this wasn't their usual one-upmanship. Something's wrong."

Dad's expression turned thoughtful, and a little sad. "Hmm. Well, don't turn yourself inside out about it, chickadee. Let them figure it out and stay out of firing range."

"I'll try."

She trudged upstairs for a quick shower, waving at her mother, who was rummaging in the storage closet at the front of the upper hallway. Probably looking for photo albums. She and Mrs. Madison liked to coo and weep over baby pictures when everyone got together for the holidays, musing about how *big* the kids were. How *grown up*. It was sweet…and kind of embarrassing. Especially since Luke was in college. They weren't children anymore.

Now, she simply had to prove it.

Chapter Five

Parker avoided looking at Luke as much as humanly possible while helping Mom set the table for dinner. Candles glowed, tall and elegant in their crystal holders, and she'd pulled out all the stops with linen tablecloths and a flower centerpiece ordered from her favorite florist in downtown Aspen. She was even wearing dress pants and a nice top instead of her usual sweater and jeans.

And now she was fixing the silverware he'd just laid on the table. Apparently they were a millimeter out of alignment. "Mom, it's just the Millers. Not a state dinner."

"It's their first night in town, and I want it to be perfect." She flashed him a smile. "I've missed Jen and Brian so much. I imagine it's nice to have Zoey back, too."

Her tone sounded expectant. Wait, did she know something? The knowing look in her eye said she did. Crap.

He used the excuse of folding a napkin to avoid looking at her. What was it about mothers and their relationship-

ESP? "Yeah. I love it when Miller's in town."

"Of course he does. Peanut Butter is incomplete without Jelly," Luke said, putting the last pot in the dishwasher. He stole a stuffed mushroom from the tray on the counter, narrowly avoiding a slap on the hand from Mom. "What?"

"Those are for our guests." The doorbell rang and Mom clapped. "They're here!"

"Does that mean I can eat the mushrooms now?" Luke called at her back as she raced to the door.

"Dude, really?" Parker muttered. "Can't you wait thirty seconds?"

"Why wait when something's right in front of you—that's what I always say."

Luke's tone was mischievous, and Parker's eyes narrowed. "What the hell does that mean?"

His brother popped a mushroom into his mouth and raised his hands as if to say, "Sorry, can't tell you."

Excited voices filled the house—Mom and Mrs. Miller talking about Mom's latest reno project, Dad teasing Mr. Miller about how bad the Cowboys looked this year. Zoey rounded the corner into the kitchen and Parker's jaw dropped. She had on tight jeans and a sweater, with her hair and makeup done. She never dressed up for dinner, and he'd never minded, but…

Damn she looked hot.

She waved a hand toward the living room. "You'd think it's been ten years since they've seen each other."

Luke swallowed the mushroom and smiled at her. "They're so cute at that age."

Zoey laughed. "Yeah? Get ready to hear that phrase all night, big boy. Mom brought photo albums with her."

Parker and Luke groaned in unison, which set them all off laughing.

"How're your legs?" Parker asked. "Think you'll be able

to board tomorrow?"

"Hey, don't think you're getting out of showing off for me." She put her hands on her hips like an angry playground monitor. "I'll be just fine tomorrow."

"I'll bring some Advil anyway, hotshot."

They stared at each other down, grinning, before Zoey said, "Point taken."

"Bring the Advil." Luke grabbed another mushroom and toasted them with it. "'Cause, bro, I think *you'll* need it after trying to keep up with me."

Great, here we go again. Could Luke lay off for one night? "If you're suggesting I'm going to wipe out tomorrow, think again. I've been home since the parks opened—you haven't. I have two weeks on you."

"And I have two *years* on you, little man." Luke puffed his chest out, looking smug, which struck Parker as stupid since he was taller. "I was boarding while you were in bunny class with Z here."

To his surprise, Zoey jumped to his rescue. "Maybe, but you taught us everything you know, which means Parker might have tricks up his sleeve you don't."

Heat spread across his chest and up the back of his neck. After the flirting earlier, it was nice to see Zoey stick up for him. "And I'm only one here smart enough to wear my helmet."

Zoey rolled her eyes. "I feel like I can't move my head in one."

Luke gave Zoey a fist bump. "And I think they look stupid. No sense in preparing for a fall that won't happen."

"You wear them to Boardercross," Parker said.

"Yeah, because that's more like roller derby than pure downhill. I don't need one for everyday stuff."

Parker sighed. "Don't come crying to me when your eyeball falls out, then."

Zoey and Luke exchanged looks and Parker gave them both a wicked grin. "Totally happened to a guy last year at one of the Snowmass Big Air Friday Nights. Hit his cheekbone and face so hard, his eye socket lost pressure and his eyeball fell out. I swear—I saw it happen. Helmets, children. Helmets."

Luke stared at the mushroom in his hands. "Think I'll throw this away."

He staggered off, face green, but Zoey shuddered with morbid glee. "You tell the most disgusting stories."

"Is that a clue you want more?" He knew full well she would. The two of them had spent hours as kids sneaking horror movies in her game room. The gorier, the more she shrieked…and the more she liked it.

"Yes, but wait until Luke's back." She chuckled. "Did you see his face? He's such a weenie."

"Remember that time he passed out when he cut his hand? Dude only needed two stitches!"

They both dissolved into silent laughter. Luke came back in and eyed them. Parker swallowed his amusement and asked, "All better?"

"Wait, about your story," Zoey said, her eyes gleaming with mischief. "What did you do?"

Parker sobered. He hadn't known the guy, but had felt for him tremendously. "I helped push the crowd out of the way so the medics could get to him."

"Wonder what happened to the eyeball?" Zoey tapped her chin with her finger, and Luke swallowed hard.

"You kids ready for dinner?" Mom called.

"Not anymore," Luke muttered, and Zoey giggled into her hand.

A pang hit Parker's chest. He liked teasing Luke, but this was probably over the line. "Just don't think about it. Trust me, you're still hungry. You just have to turn your brain off."

"Yeah?" Luke smirked. "Tell me, bro. How do you do it?"

Okay, maybe it wasn't so over the line after all.

Mom bustled into the kitchen, followed by Zoey's parents. Jen Miller was an older version of her daughter, right down to the blue eyes and blond hair. Brian Miller was a hulk of a guy—six-five, most of it muscle. To look at them, you'd see a socialite and her square-jawed bodyguard. In reality, Brian had founded a dot.com right out of college that he then sold for millions.

When he stopped to think about it—how the Millers were worth half a billion—it was kind of hard to believe. Zoey was as down-to-earth as any normal girl, not affected by her wealth, or her looks. His own parents were doing just fine. They owned a high-end ski gear line, which always ensured Parker had the best of everything, and allowed them to live in high-rent Aspen year round. But the Millers? They were a whole other kind of wealthy. Hell, Zoey drove a new BMW to school.

"Parker!" Jen stepped forward and gave him a hug, while Brian shook Luke's hand. "It's so nice to see you, honey."

He squirmed at her warm, affectionate tone. More affectionate than usual, anyway. Did she know how he felt about her daughter, too? Wait, had his mom said something? From the fond, conspiratorial twinkle in her eye, he thought she might have.

She turned to Luke next, and while her greeting was warm, it lacked a note that Parker's had.

Yeah…she knew.

They settled into their usual places around his family's huge kitchen table—the Dads at one end, the Moms at the other, with Zoey and Parker sharing a side of the middle, across from Luke. In the early days, this arrangement had been to entertain the two youngest. Later, it was to keep a twelve-year-old Luke and a ten-year-old Parker from trying to steal food off each other's plates. Now, it was simply tradition, and no one had to be told where to sit. Parker liked it that way, especially since it meant Zoey was to his left for every meal they shared.

"So, Zoey?" Parker's dad asked. "Any word on college, yet?"

She picked at her chicken. "I'm accepted to Texas, Arizona State, and Colorado State, but I haven't decided."

"Yet," her mother corrected. "But she will soon."

"Yes, mother, she will." Zoey's tone was caustic and she curled in on herself.

Parker frowned. He'd thought she was going to Colorado State with him. They'd talked about it a few years ago. Since when had she applied to Arizona State? UT made sense—that's where all four of their parents had gone. Their moms had been sorority sisters and best friends. So, when his mom fell in love with his dad, she fixed Jen up with his best friend: Brian.

But why was Zoey applying to ASU?

There was only one reason.

Luke.

He glanced up at his brother and the corner of Luke's mouth twitched. He hadn't missed that exchange, probably tallying it as another reason to make a play for Zoey. Parker fought a glare. It'd be a cold day in Hell before he'd let that happen.

He nudged Zoey's shoulder lightly. "You know, if you go to Colorado State, we can board every weekend during the season."

"I don't want to talk about it," she muttered.

Nobody talked much after that.

Once they finished the dishes, Parker finally couldn't take the silence. "Miller, talk to me."

She sighed. "It's nothing."

"No, 'it' cratered dinner." He put his hands on her shoulders. "Tell me what's wrong."

"Let's go upstairs first." She glanced toward the living room, where the parents were chatting quietly in front of the huge stone fireplace. The dads were having a post-dinner scotch, and the moms had their heads leaned together, urgently discussing something. When his mom caught him looking, she started—guilty, he thought. Yeah, they'd been talking about Zoey.

"Fine by me." He led her to the stairs at the back of the kitchen to avoid making her walk past their parents to the front staircase. The back stairs let out at the end of the upstairs hallway, across from their media room. It was empty—Luke had scarfed down his dinner, then disappeared upstairs without saying what he was up to. From the chuckles coming through his bedroom door, Parker suspected Luke was on Snapchat, checking out his groupies.

Zoey settled onto the battered couch, and he sat next to her so he could wrap an arm around her shoulders. Two years ago, that gesture would've merely been for comfort or in friendship. Tonight, he was hyperaware of the smell of her shampoo—something light, that reminded him of summer— the softness of her body leaning into his, and the feel of her breath against his neck when she rested her head on his shoulder.

Then he realized she was crying. He'd been checking her out, and she was *crying*. He was a total asshole.

He tightened his arm around her. "What's going on with your mom?"

"Nothing." She sniffled. "Really, it's not her. My parents are normal like always. It's just that I can't decide where I want to go to school, and they're in this huge hurry about it.

Like they can't wait for me to leave the house."

Parker rested his cheek against the crown of her head. "You know that's not true."

"I know, I know." She sighed heavily, and her breath made goose bumps rise on his neck. Would she notice? Wouldn't that be great? *Um, Zoey, sorry about all the college drama, but you're really turning me on right now. Scratch that—you turn me on all the time.*

He shook that thought off. Wrong time, wrong place. "So what's the real problem?"

"The real problem is I'm still trying to figure out who I really am. Class President Barbie aside, I do like my life back in Texas. There are days when I wonder if I should go to UT and join a sorority and major in broadcast media—turn into a five o'clock news anchor. But then I realize how much of myself I'll lose if I give in and go the easy route."

Man, that sounded familiar—he could always have her for a friend, if only he settled for the easy way. "What's the tough route?"

"I have no idea—that's the problem. How can I decide what I really want—where I want to go to school, what I want to study—when I'm not sure who I really am?"

"I know who you are," he whispered, stroking her hair. "You're my Zoey, and that means you can do everything."

She snuggled against him. "I like that you think I can. It makes me believe it."

"I believe it, too."

"Thanks. You know, there are days I want to major in something completely wild, like botany." She looked up at him, a challenge in her eyes. "Or liberal arts."

His lips twitched. "Really? You want to major in Humanities?"

"Stupid, right?" She sighed and settled back onto his shoulder. "My parents really want me at UT, but it doesn't *feel* right. So I applied to the schools where you and Luke are, just for something different, knowing they wouldn't argue."

"Come to Colorado State with me." The words came out in a rush, with an urgency he hadn't meant to let through. "I'll study architecture, and you'll study plants or words or basket weaving, and we'll snowboard every weekend together."

She pulled away to smile at him. "That sounds nice, but I have to decide this for me. Understand?"

He did, but was disappointed anyway. This wasn't the time to declare his love—if she wanted to figure out her future for herself, maybe he had to go about this another way. Maybe he needed to win her over. Hmm…

"What are you thinking about?" Zoey was full-on grinning now. "You have this faraway look on your face."

"Oh, it's nothing. I was just thinking…uh…"

"Better stop that," Luke said from the doorway to the media room. "Might hurt your brain."

Parker cursed under his breath. Of all times for him to show. Zoey hurriedly wiped her tears away, then smiled. "So, how about those plans? You're going to hang with us, right?"

"Sorry, Z, but they're solid. Need a raincheck on movie night." He didn't sound the least bit sorry, but he said it with a possessive smile, like he didn't want her to worry so much as wait her turn. Parker seethed at the hope in her eyes, even though she'd been blown off.

"Oh, okay." She scooted away from Parker. "I'm tired anyway. Think I'll go home and get some sleep since we're going up to Snowmass in the morning. You two picking me up?"

"Of course," Luke said smoothly, before Parker could reply.

"Great. See you then."

She hurried out of the room, head down. Parker turned to Luke, suspicious…and more than a little pissed off. "What are you even doing here?"

"Just testing the waters." Luke dug a handful of popcorn out of the half-full bowl. "I'm thinking I'll take a shot."

Parker stood up, feeling dangerous and raw. "What do you mean?"

Luke turned his head at Parker's cold tone. "You know what I mean. Show Zoey a good time, see if anything happens."

Over his dead body. Seriously. "You can't."

"Why not, Park?" Luke's voice was teasing, like he knew exactly where this conversation was headed and wanted to force Parker to spill his guts. "Give me a reason why I shouldn't go after her? She's cute, she's fearless on a snowboard, and she's feisty. All things I like. It might be strange at first—"

"How long?" Parker snapped. "How long would it be before you broke her heart? Like *every other girl you've dated*. You're a player, asshole. A complete, unapologetic player with a horde of groupies, and I won't let you play with her. Not when…"

Luke cocked his head and gave Parker a keen look. "'When' what?"

Time to stop pulling punches. "When I've been in love with her for damn near a year."

"A year? More like two." Luke laughed, sharp and vicious. "I see how you look at her."

Parker's face flamed. "If you knew, why didn't you say anything?"

"Why would I? It was your business. But I could ask the same question—why haven't you told her?" His brother shook his head. "Oh, don't tell me. You were waiting for the 'right time.' Let me tell you something, bro—the right time is always right now. You wait, and someone else will blow your shot. I know *you* see how she looks at *me*. She'll pick me if you don't give it your all, kid."

"Yeah, I see. But you're a predator when it comes to girls."

Parker's fists clenched. "Zoey will realize that eventually once she gets a good hard look at the real guy, and not the big brother she's looked up to for years."

"Prove it." Luke's eyes sparkled, like this was all one big game. "I bet I can win her over before you can."

Parker's blood boiled. "You don't even want her. Why would you even suggest something so…so…stupid?"

"Because I can, and you know I love a good bet." Luke rubbed his hands together like a supervillain crafting a plan. "Now, being the nice guy I am, I promise not to fight dirty… well, not *that* dirty. I'm willing to give you a clear shot. She'll probably still pick me, but you deserve a fighting chance."

Parker clenched his jaw. Luke promised not to get in *his* way? Like it was some kind of favor, like he was tossing his little brother a bone because there was no way Parker could possibly convince a girl to notice him if Luke was in the picture. And now that the gauntlet was thrown, Luke wouldn't take no for an answer—he was going to go after Zoey for the hell of it, just to force Parker's hand.

"If Zoey finds out we have a deal she's going to walk out on both of us."

"Which is why we aren't going to tell her. This deal is man-to-man." He leaned close. "Or are you scared you'll lose?"

His brother wanted a fight? He'd get one—and Parker wasn't about to make any promises about sportsmanlike behavior. He was in this to win the heart of the girl he loved, just like he'd planned before Luke showed up. It wasn't a game to him, not one bit. He was going to fight—dirty, hard, madly—and Luke would be smart get to out of *his* way.

"I'm not scared. Not even a little bit." Crossing his arms over his chest, he said, "It's a deal. Let the best Madison win."

Chapter Six

ZOEY

Zoey trudged up the stairs in her dark house, tears wet on her cheeks. Again. She *hated* crying, but she was doing a lot of it lately. Her parents were bugging her about college because they cared, she knew that. They just wanted her to decide so they could plan, because planning made them happy. But she couldn't decide…not until she knew if it could work with Luke or not. Because if she was totally honest, *he* was the reason she couldn't decide where to go to school, even though she knew a boy was a *really* stupid reason to choose a university.

Hence…tears.

Parker had been so sweet, talking to her about it and really listening. He got why she was struggling with the decision, at least the parts she was willing to admit. What was he thinking about, though, right before Luke came in? His features had softened, and whatever it was, it was a *good* thought. Maybe she should spend her energy investigating that instead of moping about Luke all night. He was going boarding with them in the morning, and she'd have him—both of them—to herself all day.

So what *had* made Parker so happy? Did he have a girlfriend? He didn't talk about that stuff much, except for the hysterical laughing fit they'd both had sophomore year when they realized they'd lost their virginity in the exact same week. Then they'd sulked together because the people they'd been with hadn't really been the right ones. Did he finally find the "right one?"

And if he had, would this new love take him out of Zoey's life?

Her face flamed. Ugh, she wasn't going to be *that* girl. If Parker had found love, she'd be happy for him.

Mostly.

She flipped on the light in her bedroom upstairs and automatically looked out the window. Parker's bedroom window was right across from hers, a fact they'd exploited a lot when they were younger—tin can phones, secret codes, and walkie-talkies before they had iPhones. Those were the golden days of Aspen, when everything was simple and nothing but fun.

Tonight, Parker's window was dark. Just as well. She shut her blinds and went to put on her pajamas, before crawling onto her bed to stretch out her legs and back in anticipation of the muscle aches she was sure to have tomorrow. She really shouldn't have taken those last two runs, but Luke had been very persuasive. Parker had glowered at Luke when he thought she wasn't looking.

Which created another problem...was Parker really establishing himself as her guardian/chaperone? How would he take it if she was successful with Luke? It wouldn't change their friendship...at least, she hoped it wouldn't.

Yeah, and if Parker's found a girl, you can't let it change your friendship, either.

She snuggled into the covers and reached to turn out the light, but her phone buzzed. A Snapchat notification…from Luke.

Letting out a slow breath, she opened it up. Luke had taken a picture of himself in the front seat of the Jeep, hand over his heart. "Sorry to ditch you tonight."

After that picture cycled through, there was a second, with Luke giving her a big dose of sexy grin. "I'll make it up to you tomorrow."

Zoey's heart stuttered. He'd apologized for not staying with her. Did that mean she was making progress?

Her phone buzzed a third time, and she snatched it up eagerly, but it wasn't Luke. This time it was a text from Paige, full of blushing smiley faces.

Zoey shot upright in bed, laughing as tears sprang to her eyes for a different reason. Her thumbs fumbled the phone as she typed out a quick text.

Z: *And?!!!*

P: **snort* Your house is fine. Mail's in, porch light is on.*

Zoey growled at the evasion. Paige knew damn well what she was asking. *Uh huh, and what else?*

P: *Thanks for giving me your key.*

She smiled at the phone. She'd given Paige the key to her house under the guise of telling her parents how responsible her friend would be about bringing in the mail and checking on everything, but she had an ulterior motive—giving her and Ben a very private place, away from Paige's still-overprotective mom.

Z: *That didn't take long—we've only been gone a day!*

P: *The tension was killing us. Ha!*

Z: *Are you and Prince Geek a little less, um, stressed now?*

P: *A LOT less stressed.*

Z: *Details?*

P: *No way.*

Z: *Oh, God. You didn't use my room did you?*

P: *No! Eww…that would be so…so…*

Z: *Exactly. I'm so happy for you guys, though.*

P: *How's Aspen?*

Zoey stared at the screen, chewing her lip. How did she answer that question? Paige didn't know about the Madison boys, or even that Zoey loved Aspen. She thought it was some drag-along vacation Zoey was forced to take twice a year. She kept this part of her life private—very private—for a reason. She felt like her life was always on display, and Aspen was the one thing she got to keep to herself. She wasn't selfish about much, but her hideaway from Alderwood needed to stay hers, and only hers, for a little while longer.

Would Paige understand when Zoey finally told her the truth? Probably. It's not every day you find out your best friend has been living a secret life. Maybe once she and Luke were together, it would be easier.

Z: *Fine. Good snow this year.*

P: *Good. Miss you!*

Z: *Miss you, too. Say hi to Geek Charming for me.*

P: *Done. XOXO*

Zoey set the phone on her nightstand and turned off the lamp. She *was* happy for Paige, and for Ben, but the thought of the two of them together, safe in their own joy, made her heart hurt. She was lonely.

No one at home would believe that for a moment. The Great Zoey Miller...lonely? Pshaw. How could that be true? She was surrounded by people—watched, admired... *worshiped.*

Ugh, that word was cringe-worthy, but she knew guys said it. The idea made her ill.

So, yeah. She was lonely. It was a self-imposed loneliness, to be sure, from hiding behind the disguise of a girl who was always polished, with everything together all the time. How was she ever supposed to be free with a guy? Every guy she'd tried to date saw her as a trophy.

If it bothered her, though, why didn't she feel comfortable enough to show her Dallas friends what Parker saw every day? Why did she go on being what everyone expected?

Did she really crave the attention that much?

Speaking of cringe-worthy...damn. *Oh, look, the poor, pretty rich girl. What kind of problems can* she *have?*

Maybe she was being selfish for being sad. Maybe her problems weren't as important as everyone else's. Maybe she was right to keep them hidden. No one would believe how insecure she felt deep down inside. How, when she went home after school and took off her shoes and makeup, she sighed with relief to have made it through another day. *That's* what college meant to her: a fresh start. To go somewhere no one knew her, having the chance to wear leggings, a T-shirt, and flip-flops to class. No armor.

Just Zoey.

She sighed in the dark and rolled over. That day was coming soon. She just had to hang on until then.

Sunday morning dragged on for *days*. The boys never got up early, because the mountain was always *right there* waiting for them. Zoey, on the other hand, had fourteen short days of snowboarding, and she wanted to make the most of it.

Mom laughed when Zoey dropped her phone on the kitchen table and stuck her tongue out at it. "Sweetheart, it's only nine-thirty. Let them sleep in one day, okay?"

"I know I should, but I feel like the clock's ticking." She crossed her arms and slumped in her chair. Wanting to see Luke made her feel crazy. She didn't like it. Yesterday, she'd flirted with him shamelessly, hanging on his every word like the groupies she despised.

Not to mention the fact that she'd done her hair and makeup both yesterday *and* this morning, in hopes that he'd notice. Was trying to win his heart worth keeping up the act she put on back home long enough to get his attention? Was it worth holding off on a college decision?

She hoped so.

She wished she could count on Luke to act the way Parker had about her college dilemma, but she wasn't sure she could—that would force her to admit she'd only applied to ASU because he was there. Yes, Luke made her heart race, but would he think she was silly for basing her future on the chance he could love her back?

"If you're that worried about getting enough snowboarding in, why not go up by yourself? You know that mountain like the back of your hand. It's not like you need a Madison to guide you around," Mom said.

Sure, that was an option, but boarding alone was…boring. It wasn't like she didn't know how to keep herself company — she just didn't want to if she didn't have to. Especially not after last night, considering how down in the dumps she'd been. She needed a friend to make her world sparkle…or a Luke to make her pulse race.

Her phone buzzed on the table, saving her from answering her mother, and she ran to grab it.

P: *I'm up, I'm up. Someone's impatient.*

Zoey sighed. It wasn't Luke answering her hail, but if anyone could cheer her up, it was Parker. *Yes, I am. We're burning daylight! Wake up Luke, and let's go.*

A pause. *Luke's totally crashed. I heard him come in around three. So you're stuck with me if you want to go now.*

A kernel of doubt gnawed at her. What was he doing out with friends until three? He'd told her he was going to make it up to her today, and she thought that meant getting an early start at Snowmass.

Knowing Luke, they picked up some girls. He couldn't go anywhere without a coven forming to follow him around. He often blamed his "natural charm" — and there was some truth to that. How could she compete if every girl in a five-mile radius wanted him, too?

She rolled her eyes. Pouting wasn't going to do any good. She'd have to work harder at making him notice her, that's all.

Z: *Sucks to be him. Meet you outside in twenty.*

P: *At your service.*

He was such a goof. Grinning, she spun around to her mom. "Parker's up. He'll go with."

Mom smiled into her coffee cup. "You can always rely on Parker to be there, can't you?"

"Yep." And if he could help her convince Luke to meet up with them later, all the better.

Chapter Seven

PARKER

Parker's hands shook a little as he zipped up his jacket. This was it—he had a whole morning alone at Snowmass with Zoey. Luke could sleep in all he wanted—after the bet last night, Parker was going to use this chance to his best advantage.

Zoey was waiting for him by his car when he came outside. He shut the door nice and quiet, to make sure he didn't disturb Sleeping Beauty upstairs.

"I've been waiting for you guys to wake up *forever*," she said, climbing into the Land Rover. "What was Luke doing out last night until three?"

Parker didn't answer, and slammed the tailgate shut. He knew full well what Luke had been doing, and he was still pissed. The "guy friends" he'd mentioned to Zoey included three girls. He'd sent Parker a snap saying, "Wish you were here!" and one of the girls in the picture was wound around him so tight, Parker wanted to suggest they get a room. So, not only had he bet Parker he could win Zoey over first, he did it on a night he had a date — a date he lied about to the very girl he was trying to steal.

His head pounded just thinking about it, and his chest felt tight with unspent anger. He could really go for punching the sand out of a bag right now, but the mountain would help just as much. And he wouldn't hurt Zoey by mentioning it, but he wasn't going to do Luke any favors, either.

When he hopped into the driver's seat, Zoey repeated the question. "Where did he go last night?"

Parker strangled the steering wheel with his hands. "To a party at a guy's house. That's what it sounds like."

"Hope he didn't drive home drunk," she murmured, staring out the window.

At that, he almost told her. She was so concerned about where Luke had been and how he was now, that she totally missed the point. "I don't know. He's usually smarter than that, though."

"Good." She finally smiled at him. "So what are we going to do first? Since Luke's not here, maybe we should wait on going up to the Cirque."

"That's fine." Changing the plan didn't mean he couldn't take her on a little adventure though. Especially if it distracted her from Luke. "Let's go up to the High Alpine, take some of the diamonds up there, if you're up for it."

She nodded, considering. "Oh, I'm up for it."

He gave her an appraising smile. "Good. I'm in the mood for some speed."

"I thought that was Luke's line."

He managed to keep the smile on his face as he leaned over into her seat. "Not always."

Her sides were shaking with an effort not to laugh. She fluttered her eyelashes and fanned her face. "Ooh la la, you better show me something good, big boy."

A fire raged in his chest, spreading a flush up his torso and around to the back of his neck. He *almost* had her. "Will do, Miller. Will do."

She giggled and pushed him back toward his seat. "Put your money where your mouth is, then."

He put the car in gear. "I intend to."

Parker stood at the gate to Grinder, a straight shot trail that sent skiers and boarders alike careening down the mountain as fast as they liked. They hadn't run this trail together for two years, mainly because Luke thought it was boring. Parker was out to prove his brother wrong.

Zoey peered over the edge. "It's steeper than I remembered."

"It's a great ride. Promise."

"Okay." She frowned and stood next to him. "Are we racing?"

"Nope, just doing a mad dash for fun." He pulled on his goggles and tightened the strap to his helmet. "You ready?"

She jammed her cap down on her head. "As I'll ever be."

He heard the doubt in her voice. No matter how bold she was with Luke, Parker knew steep runs made her nervous. He was out to prove that she *could* do it. "You'll do great. I'll stick close by, okay?"

She nodded, and they went over the edge together. The first bit wasn't very steep, but they gained speed quickly. The sunshine was bright on the snow, almost blinding. Both of them had protective eyewear, but it was still a challenge. Parker stayed behind and above Zoey, making sure she was doing okay. When she squealed, he sped around her and jumped to turn one-hundred-eighty degrees so he could face her.

She had a manic smile on her face, like she couldn't decide

if this was the most awesome thing she'd ever done, or she was about to have a stroke.

Parker moved closer and gave her a thumbs up. "You can do this. Stay low and go."

He bent his knees, mimicking for her to do the same. They streaked down the hill, her screaming all the way. By the time they reached the bottom, her hands were shaking as she pulled off her cap, but she was laughing.

"Well?" he asked, skidding to a halt next to her. "Was I right?"

"You were right." She leaned against his arm. "That was almost as exhilarating as sex. Let's go again!"

She scampered off toward the lifts, leaving Parker stranded, flustered, and unable to get the idea of exhilarating sex out of his head.

By the time they made it home, Zoey had plunged down Grinder four more times, and hit three other black diamond trails. Her cheeks were pink and her eyes shone as they drove home. Her hair was down again, but she'd let it get all windblown, and she looked relaxed for the first time since she'd arrived.

Chest swelling with pride, he asked, "Did I show you a good time or what?"

"It was the *best* time." She bounced in her seat like she was seven again. "That was so much fun."

"See, we don't have to have Luke with us to have fun."

That slipped out, wishful thinking maybe, and Zoey's crooked frown make him curse his stupid mouth. If he wanted her to forget about Luke, why the hell did he keep saying his brother's name?

"We probably should apologize for going without him,"

she said.

"No."

The word came out hard, forceful, and Zoey recoiled. "Why not?"

Parker clenched his jaw to keep from sounding like a cornered bobcat—all teeth and claws. "Because he was tired, and probably didn't want to come with us anyway. If he'd wanted to go, he wouldn't have stayed out until three, knowing full well we were going to Snowmass this morning."

Her shoulders tensed. "And how would you feel if he and I left you behind because you overslept?"

She made it sound like a challenge, and it hit him where it hurt. "I'd feel abandoned."

She crossed her arms and stared out the window. "That's right. So we'll apologize."

But when they made it to his place for dinner, Luke was hanging out with the dads in the living room, watching a bowl game and laughing.

He looked up when they came in. "You two have fun?"

There wasn't a single bit of jealousy in his tone. In fact, he sounded a lot like their dad asking Parker how a date went. Not that he'd dated anyone since Zoey stole his heart, but still. Could he be any more condescending, especially since Parker had one-upped him by taking Zoey out all day? It was like he didn't care one bit.

Worse, it was like Parker spending the whole day with Zoey didn't *worry* him one bit.

Zoey crumpled at Luke's reaction. She probably wished Luke had been heartbroken that they'd left him, instead of perfectly happy in front of the TV. She shrugged. "Yeah. Where were you?"

"My plans changed. Sorry, Z. I thought Parker could stand in for me." Luke's mouth twitched with a hidden smirk. "Bro, don't you know how to entertain a guest at all?"

"We had a good time." Which was true—Zoey had said so until she realized Luke didn't miss her all day. Which blew. Parker narrowed his eyes at Luke, wishing eye-lasers were a thing. He'd melt Luke's eyebrows right off. See who gloated then. "Zoey ran down Grinder, did great."

"Grinder, pah." Luke shook his head. "No obstacles, just a hill. We definitely should go up on The Cirque tomorrow. That's a trail that'll make you cry for your mama. How about it, Z? You up for that?"

She lifted her head and met his gaze dead on. "I'm up for anything."

Luke smiled when her tone challenged his, and a spark passed between them. Parker groaned inwardly. Fine, let them have a moment. He was too strung out to keep up his game face.

"I'm going to clean up." Parker held in the extra-intense glare he had reserved for Luke and stomped out of the room.

Tomorrow, he'd try harder.

Chapter Eight

ZOEY

The sun was peeking over the horizon when Zoey bounced downstairs dressed in fleece leggings, thick socks, and a thermal top, ready to slip into her ski gear. It was barely past seven, and the Cirque's lift didn't open until ten, but she knew the boys would be by soon. She'd gone to bed pissed that Luke was fine skipping out on her, but he'd said they were definitely on today, so she couldn't stay angry.

The Sky Cab opened at eight, and she'd made sure they understood her displeasure at waiting until late morning yesterday. Today, they'd want to hit whatever trails were open until they could go up top. The Cirque Headwall was a series of nasty trails, black diamonds, doubles, and extremes, that started at the highest point the resort would allow you to go. Legally, anyway. There were boarders who went *way* off trail to find the scariest rides they could, but she didn't agree with that. Good way to get yourself killed, without any chance of someone finding you.

She hummed while she made coffee, then went to pull her hair back in a ponytail. For a second, she debated if she should wear it down again, on Luke's account, but if they were taking rough trails, better to have it out of the way. When she came back to the kitchen, Mom was staring longingly at the coffeepot, still wearing her pajamas and a bathrobe.

"Have I told you today what a great kid you are?" She gave Zoey a half-asleep smile. "Coffee, already on the go? And you're dressed…early day on Snowmass, huh?"

Zoey smiled and helped herself to a protein bar. "The boys are taking me up on Cirque."

Mom's eyebrows rose. "Be careful."

"I will. I can't vouch for those two knuckle-draggers, though."

"Oh, I think Parker's plenty careful." Mom chuckled. "I'm worried about Luke."

"Don't be," Zoey said, feeling the need to defend him. "He takes his shredding very seriously."

"That's the only thing," Mom muttered into her coffee mug.

Not a glowing endorsement. What would she do if she knew Zoey wanted to date him? Probably try to talk her out of it. That wouldn't stop her though. She deserved to forge her own happiness, to *decide*, to be herself. If Mom didn't like it now, she'd learn to.

The doorbell rang, and she hopped up to get it before Mom could start another lecture. She flung open the front door, and the boys stood on the doorstep, already dressed for the day out, Luke in his trademark red ski gear, and Parker in blue. She loved the cut of the Madisons' ski gear line, especially on guys. It stretched across their shoulders, but was cut close, to emphasize everything that looked good on a guy. So hot. And the red made Luke stand out, even as a tiny dot on the mountainside.

No one spoke for a second, then she realized what was wrong—her top had pulled up a little when she leaned against the door. A strip of skin was visible, and both of them were staring at it.

Luke's gaze thrilled her. Parker…he was staring, too, but why? He'd seen her in a swimsuit for years. His gaze made her flush and she tugged the shirt down, forgetting to be alluring for Luke in her confusion. "Uh, sorry. I was talking to Mom and lost track of time. Come on in."

"No worries," Luke drawled behind her as she led them to the kitchen. "View's nice."

Her ears burned, especially when she heard a thump and a shuffle of steps, along with Luke's muttered, "Stop it, asshat." Parker must've shoved Luke into a wall. Flirting was going to be so much harder with him around. Was that why he stared a moment ago? Because he was disgusted with her? It was an accident, but what if he thought she'd done it on purpose?

That bothered her.

"Morning, boys." Mom's hand fluttered to her mussed hair. "Sorry for the bedhead."

"It's all right, Miss Jen," Parker said, as Zoey hurried to the mudroom, keeping her back to everyone. "You're practically our mom. Bedhead's totally cool."

Mom laughed, and started grilling them both about school. Zoey closed the mudroom door behind her and leaned against it, listening to the half-audible murmur of voices. This morning was already off to a weird start, and she was so flustered she needed a minute to chill.

After a few deep breaths, she gathered ski gear together. Her lime green jacket with the leaf pattern on the sleeves—a Madison exclusive designed just for her, and a gift from Tina and Jason last Christmas—was her favorite piece. She had other jackets, but she never wore them anymore. She had a pair of matching bibs, and her parents had, on a whim, bought her a pair of black boots with her name airbrushed in green on the side. She'd proclaimed them cheesy, and hoped she never ran into anyone from school on the mountain, but she wore the boots all the time, anyway.

Ready, she smoothed down her jacket with shaking fingers. She couldn't go on being embarrassed around Luke. She had to turn on the heat, and finish what she started. She could do this. She *could*.

She grabbed her board and flung open the door. "All right, boys, let's go show the tourists how to shred."

Chapter Nine

All Parker could think about on the ride to Snowmass was that strip of skin Zoey had accidentally flashed. He knew it wasn't on purpose, although Luke's weak attempt at flirting made him think Luke thought she had. His brother knew *nothing* about Zoey. She hated flaunting her body, and any time it happened, it was inadvertent. From the way her ears had turned pink, he knew she felt weird about it, too.

That's mostly why he'd shoved Luke into the wall. Although, seeing him trip over his own feet was pretty amusing.

Zoey's voice broke into his thoughts. "Which trail do you guys want to run from The Cirque?"

"Headwall," Luke said before Parker could answer. "Great natural jibs up there. Moguls, too. Not like that manmade crap on the terrain parks."

Parker bristled. The terrain parks were *his* turf, and Luke loved to poke fun at his "little skater hobby." He knew the only reason his brother teased him about it was because he wasn't all that good at ramps or rails. No, Luke was built to shred fast, to go off trail into deep snow, and to jump moguls like he knew what jumping really was. He wouldn't be caught dead trying to take the big air ramps down at the park.

And he probably thought Parker wouldn't, either. Wait a minute…

"Sounds good," Parker said, biting back a sly smile. "We can go down to Snowmass Park tomorrow. They have a 20-foot kicker this year and a lot of new features."

"Parks are for wusses." Luke waved a hand. "You want to jump, tackle a natural ramp."

"We'll do both," Zoey said, and Parker's heart soared. "I know full well you know how to ride a rail, Luke. Just like I know Parker can tackle a mogul."

True, but can Luke ride a down-flat-down pipe, or a stair rail? No, he can't. Parker bit back another smile. Time to ride and shine. And plot. Definitely time to plot.

"So, bro, you hear that they're having an amateur slopestyle competition on Wednesday?" Parker asked, all innocence. "Prize money's two-grand."

Even from the back seat, Parker could see Luke's hands tighten on his steering wheel. "Is our company sponsoring it?"

Nice attempt at getting out of this. "Nope. Means you can enter. The deadline's today."

"Me?" Luke's voice went up at the end, and Parker almost laughed—he totally had him. "What about you?"

Time to lower the boom. "Oh, but I already have."

Zoey whipped around in her seat, grinning. "Are you serious? I've always wanted to watch you guys compete." She turned to Luke. "Please say you'll do it. *Please.*"

Parker thought he could hear his brother's teeth crack as he clenched his jaw. "Yeah, sounds fun."

Oh, yes…yes, it sure did. After Wednesday afternoon,

Zoey would be sure to give him—and not Luke—a solid look. He'd win that two-grand and buy her something nicer than the little charm bracelet he'd reserved as her Christmas gift. It would be perfect.

The parking lot was already filling up when they arrived, and they wasted no time pulling their gear from Luke's trunk and heading for the tram. Even though it was Monday, a lot of weekenders had stayed over, and the lines for the lifts were long.

Zoey shifted from foot to foot, full of restless energy. Luke wasn't paying her any attention, so Parker took advantage. He sidled up to her, making sure to keep Luke in front of them, where he'd have a good view of the college girls ahead of them in line. That should keep him occupied for a while.

"How are your legs today?" he asked in a low voice. "You ready for Headwall?"

She smiled. It was muted, but she was smiling, and that's what mattered. "I'm fine—nothing a couple of Advil and a hot shower couldn't cure."

Zoey…in the shower. Now *that* was an image he'd have stuck in his head all day. He leaned a little closer. "Good to hear it. You know, I worry about you."

"Why?" She slid under his arm to lean against his side. "I'm okay."

"You're my…" Crap, how did he finish this sentence? Jesus, he needed to get a grip. "You're the Jelly in this sandwich. Which makes you important. To me. I like you happy. And feisty. I like it when you're feisty best of all."

She peered up at him from beneath long lashes, her blue eyes wide. "Who, me? I'm never feisty."

The way she was looking at him hit him square in the chest. He gave her one of those slow smiles that she seemed to like so much. "What if I told you I brought a fake eyeball with me and I'm going to pretend to crash and drop it on the snow in front of Luke?"

Zoey covered her mouth with her hand, eyes alight. "You wouldn't."

"I would…but I won't today. I promise to behave."

She frowned suddenly. "What's going on with you two, anyway? You're acting like you can't stand to be around each other. I get that you're competitive, but this is worse than usual."

Now it was Parker's turn to clench his jaw. "It's not a big thing. Typical Luke."

The eyebrow raise told him she didn't believe that. "Speaking of which, he's miles ahead of us in line. How'd that happen?"

Parker turned and found Luke chatting up one of the college girls, having skipped about ten spots in the lift line. "Making friends already, looks like, and talking his way to the front of the line."

Zoey stared at her boots, her ponytail falling into her face. He nudged her. "Finished your Christmas shopping yet?"

She took a deep breath and looked up. "Yes. You?"

"Uh…"

Now she smiled. "Parker Madison. Why is it that every Christmas I have to buy your mom's gift for you?"

"You have better taste?" He gave her a sheepish grin. "Or maybe I'm hopeless?"

"Probably both."

They shuffled forward. The college girl and her friends made it to the front of the line. Just before they settled onto the lift, the girl held up her phone and mouthed, "Call me."

Luke waved at them as they ascended, but didn't hop onto the next lift. Instead, he walked back to Parker and Zoey, looking pleased with himself. Almost like he forgot he was supposedly pursuing Zoey…and then remembered.

"We go to school together," he said in excuse. "Met her

and her friends at a party last fall."

"Oh." Zoey's face brightened. "So you aren't going to ditch us after all."

"Ditch you?" Luke put a hand over his heart, wounded, and Parker glared at the ground. "Never, Z. I remembered we had a date."

"A date?" Zoey squeaked. "What did you have in mind?"

She asked it with a little flutter of eyelashes and Parker's fists clenched. She was flirting like all those girls who trailed behind Luke. This wasn't like her at all—and watching her try so hard with him made Parker a little sad. And pissed at his brother for egging her on. Capital P, fireworks, Pissed.

Luke shot Parker a cagey glance. "For you to watch me show little bro here how it's done."

"Nice," Parker muttered, scowling.

The lift line shortened. When the next quad arrived, there were only two people in front of them. Winking at Parker, Luke grabbed Zoey's hand. "Only two seats left. See you at the top!"

And, just like that, Parker was left standing on the lift platform alone.

Chapter Ten

ZOEY

Zoey felt bad, watching Parker getting smaller and smaller behind them, but *oh, my God,* she was finally alone with Luke. Maybe she should've done more with her hair. Her hands fluttered of their own accord and she had to force them into her lap.

The other two people, a pair of skiers, were engrossed in conversation—in French. Canadian, most likely, based on the Maple Leafs sticker on the man's helmet. Good, then they wouldn't try to make small talk.

The Two Creeks lift was one of the longer ones at Snowmass, which gave her plenty of time to make her move. Except her tongue had twisted itself into a knot. Is this how guys back home felt when they tried to talk to *her*? If so, she could develop some sympathy for them.

Luke, though, didn't have any problem talking. "How's your morning been, beautiful?"

She flushed. He often called her that, usually teasing, but

she felt it every single time. "Good. It's cold up here today, though."

"Let me help with that." He slipped an arm around her shoulders.

How many times had he done that when they were kids? Hundreds, but she hadn't been so keenly aware of his touch when she was twelve. She'd been more likely to shake his arm off, then. But now, she felt every millimeter of pressure of his arm against her shoulders. Her stomach fluttered. Did he mean for that to happen, or was he being friendly?

"Thanks." She let out a long breath, watching frozen mist escape her mouth to disappear on the air. "The girl in line seemed to want your number. Did you give it to her?"

"She gave me hers." He laughed. "Why? Jealous?"

Hell, yes, I am. "I'm jealous of anyone stealing my time with you and Park."

"Ah, so it *is* both of us, then?"

His voice was light, but a note of curiosity caught her ear. "Well, yeah. But I spend a ton of time with Parker. We're best friends. I feel like I don't spend enough time with you."

There. She'd practically shouted "spend time with me!" And from the faintly pleased look in his eye, he heard what she meant.

"I'm here until New Year's Eve. I'm heading back to Arizona for a party that night." He smiled at her in a way that made her ski gear feel much too warm, despite the twenty-degree temperature. "I'm all yours until then."

Her stomach swooped, as if the lift was hurtling her to earth instead of sweeping her up the mountain. "Lucky me."

The heat turned up on his smile. "You have no idea."

Oh, but she did. And she wanted to find out if she was right. "I know we said we'd go dancing Wednesday, but what about tonight? I heard about a place that does sleigh rides."

He sat back. "Sleigh rides?"

Her face flamed for a new reason—he sounded skeptical. Worse, he sounded a little amused with her. "It, um, could be stupid fun. But really, I'm up for anything."

"I think you should take Park on the sleigh ride—it sounds like something you two would enjoy. Maybe save something a little more…edgy for me."

The word edgy had promise, as did his flirtatious wink, but her stomach sank. She knew a brush off when she heard one. She forced a smile. "I'll give it some thought."

"Do that."

The lift reached the crest of its run, and she prepared to exit the chair, feeling stupid. Why had she asked a college guy to go on a *sleigh ride*? Pathetic. Was she trying too hard? Maybe that was why he was pushing her buttons, interested one second, dismissive the next—because she was acting like a silly high school girl.

Or maybe she needed to fight fire with fire. She'd ask Parker to go on that sleigh ride and they'd have a blast, and tell Luke he missed all the fun. Luke didn't like being left out—and that might capture his attention. She chewed on her bottom lip. Playing hard to get might work, and even make Luke jealous. She knew he liked a challenge, and couldn't stand being one-upped by anyone, especially when it came to girls or snowboarding.

She'd do it—she'd ask Parker to go, and see how Luke reacted to that.

They skated over to the trail's gate and waited for Parker to join them. Luke kept glancing at her out of the corner of her eye. There was interest there, she just had to find a way to stoke the fire a little bit and let the rest take its course.

Parker hopped off the lift, skating over to them as fast as he could. Behind him a group of Japanese tourists exited the lift with a lot less grace. Skiers, the lot of them. They spoke with animated hand gestures, pointing at Parker's board.

"We need to go," he said in a rush, bending to strap his back foot into the bindings. "Now. I think they want to follow me around."

The corner of Luke's mouth turned up. "Scared of a few tourists?"

With a wink at Parker, Zoey gave Luke a little shove. He wobbled a bit—the first time she'd ever seen his balance fail—but recovered and tipped over the edge. She shooed Parker next, waggling her eyebrows as the tourists closed the distance between them. He moved with more grace, and more urgency, than his brother.

Once they were gone, she paused to close her eyes and take a cleansing breath of pine-scented air. The cold seared her lungs and her brain settled. Up here, confusing boys could be forgotten. Slights could be forgiven. Up here, Zoey was free.

She waved at the tourists, and they all smiled and waved back. One, a man about her dad's age, she thought, said in passable English, "The young man. Your boyfriend?"

She wasn't sure which boy he meant, but that didn't matter: neither Madison fit that label. "No. Just a friend."

"Ah. He's a good boy. Showed us his board." The man gave her a thumbs up. "He left us, though. Would you show us how they work?"

Laughing, Zoey saluted the group and kicked over the edge. Applause followed. The tourists must not have seen a snowboarder in real life before. The guys were way ahead of her, but she could show off in Parker's place. She shredded a neat line along the trail, swooping over to take a small mogul, and landing it cleanly. She didn't like the bigger jumps, not after fracturing her arm in a nasty fall a few years back, but a little air never killed anyone…or sent them to the ER.

The wind bit at her face and sent her ponytail streaming out behind her. The *swoosh-whoosh* of her board's edge against the snow made its own music, drowning out the laughter of skiers as she flew by. She took another tiny jump, turning her body so she faced the other way, riding goofy-style. Her knees shook, but held. Her legs were relearning the feel of the board. She jumped and turned back to her dominant side, took a wide cut, and sprayed loose powder into the trees. Behind, she heard delighted yells, and knew she'd put on a good show for the tourists.

Grinning, she zipped to the bottom of the trail, cutting hard to screech to a stop right next to Parker. So, maybe her board flung a little snow into his jacket. And maybe a little of that snow went down his collar. His shout of surprise made her laugh out loud with the kind of joy she only found at Snowmass with her best friend.

Eyes narrowed, but twinkling with mischief, Parker bent down and gathered up a glove full of snow. Zoey shrieked and ducked. The snowball flew over her head…and hit something with a wet *thunk*.

"Moffer-wucker!" Luke spluttered around a face full of snow. He swiped most of it away with a gloved hand. "What was that for?"

Parker and Zoey were reduced to silent, shaking, can't-breathe-oh-my-God laughter. She wheezed in some air. "That…was for…me."

"Guess that's my good deed for the day, then," he grumbled.

"Sorry, bro. I didn't mean to plow you in the face." Parker turned away to bite back a grin, which set Zoey laughing again. "Nice look, though. Frosty eyebrows are totally your thing."

Luke heaved an annoyed sigh and scraped the snow from his eyebrows. "You two ready to go up top?"

Zoey nodded timidly. He sounded a little angry. Was he mad at her? "I'm ready for my show."

Luke's hundred-watt grin returned, but it didn't quite reach his eyes. "Good. Let's do it."

Chapter Eleven

Parker

Luke took off for the lift, assuming they'd be right behind him, but Parker turned to Zoey. "What's wrong?"

She was staring at Luke's back, her forehead wrinkled. She shook herself when he asked. "Oh, nothing."

Right. The same Nothing who was several strides ahead of them by now. "We better catch up with Luke."

They followed his trail, and Zoey, voice meek, asked, "Think he might be mad because I pushed him over the edge at the top of the trail?"

"If he's mad about that, he's an idiot." Parker nudged her shoulder with his. "You push me over the edge all the time, and I laugh it off."

She didn't look convinced.

Parker fumed as they hiked over to the Sheer Bliss lift, not bothering to hurry. Cirque was the highest point on Snowmass, so they'd have to take a second, smaller surface lift to reach the trails. His asshole brother could ride all the way to the top by himself as far as Parker was concerned.

"Do you have plans tonight?" Zoey twisted a strand of hair around a finger, a sign she was still anxious over Luke.

"Nope. You?" *Please don't say you're going out with the asshat.*

"I do…did." She frowned. "*Do*. There's a place doing sleigh rides through the woods near town. It sounded…fun."

Her tone held a tentative note, like she was scared he'd laugh or tell her it was a stupid idea. How could she even think that? He'd go on an Artic mission with her—possibly naked—if she asked. He'd go anywhere she wanted him to go.

She slowly turned red. "It's okay. We don't have—"

"I'd love to go," he said, touching her shoulder. "I've never been in a real sleigh before. It sounds fun."

Her blush faded and she gave him a grateful smile. "Good. Luke said it sounded stupid, so I wasn't sure."

She asked Luke first? That stung. On the other hand, he'd hurt Zoey's feelings, giving Parker an entire evening alone with her. On a sleigh…where it was cold. Cold encouraged snuggling. Snuggling *might* encourage other things. Second choice or not, he was going to use that time wisely.

He patted her back. "Luke wouldn't know fun if it punched him in the balls."

Zoey's laugh pealed out, and it warmed him straight through. There was a good mission: make Zoey laugh as much as possible. Her entire body changed when she was happy, from the light in her eyes, to the relaxed swing of her arms. It was like seeing the real girl climb out of a Zoey Miller costume. This girl didn't care that she waddled a little when she walked because of her bulky clothes, or that her hair was flying free from her ponytail, whipping around in the wind, where it could get caught in her lip gloss.

Hell, this girl wasn't even *wearing* lip gloss. She'd been wearing it this morning, but at some point she'd forgotten to put more on. Come to think of it, she wasn't wearing as much makeup as she had the first couple of days. Hot as she'd looked in it, he definitely preferred how she looked without it.

It's nice to see you again, real Zoey. Stay with me, okay?

That was going to be harder than he thought, though, because Luke stood outside the lift-line, waiting for them. "Where have you two been?"

Zoey wilted under his stare...and started to climb back into her untouchable Class President self by smoothing the loose strands back into her ponytail. No fucking way Parker would let that happen again.

He edged in front of her and, forcing a cheery smile, flipped Luke off. "We took our time. It's a vacation—no need to rush. Now, would letting you pelt me with a snowball cheer you up? Because, buttface, you're acting like a pissed off grizzly." He spread his arms wide. "I know I deserve it, and I'll stand right here."

Behind him, Zoey giggled and Luke gave him an annoyed wave off, not realizing—which he never did—that Parker refusing to get angry when Luke was having a tantrum diffused his mood in seconds. Huh, maybe that was his superpower.

Crisis averted, they jumped in line, Parker making sure to keep Zoey behind him so she'd be forced to ride with him. It worked, too. Even though they were on the same chair, Parker ended up between Zoey and Luke. Right where he wanted to be.

The surface lift pulled them to the Cirque gate, giving Parker a spectacular view of the trail. It had opened early, only two days ago, and the snow was smooth. Dark pines stuck out against the glistening white, as stark reminders that this was an extreme trail. Luke's element. Parker studied perfection—

practicing tricks at the terrain park over and over until he could do them on muscle memory alone. Luke, on the other hand, shredded like a demon with wings.

When Parker made it to the gate, Zoey in tow, Luke was staring down the trail with a manic gleam in his eyes. "Look at it," he breathed, like he was taking in a Picasso or a gorgeous motorcycle. "And it's all mine."

"Not exactly." Zoey's mouth turned down. "We're coming with, remember?"

Parker took a step closer to her. "You know he'll take off when he hits the steep stuff. Stick with me."

Luke rolled his eyes. "I won't. But do keep up."

And with that, Luke flung himself over the edge. Parker shrugged at Zoey. "One…two…three!"

They tipped over at the same time, Parker keeping a close eye on her. The Cirque looked so simple at first, until it took you into the trees, down steep grades, and over bumpy, knee-jarring moguls. Up here, the obstacles weren't made of metal. They were made of ice, wood, and fear.

Ahead, Luke was doing his best to show off. He took wide turns, intentionally grazing the edge of the run. He might like to ditch the trail whenever he could, but not even Luke was stupid enough to do it on The Cirque—the avalanche danger was too high. Still, he pushed the extremes, finding plenty of drops to catch air, and skimming the snow with a hand when he leaned hard into a turn.

"What a hot dog," Parker muttered. He could easily catch up, but he wasn't going to leave Zoey alone up here.

"He's a knuckle-dragging hot dog!" Zoey yelled, flying past him with a giant smile on her face. She was radiant, shining like the diamond brightness of the snow.

If that's how she wanted to play it… Parker picked up speed and caught her, hitting a mogul and catching air on the backside. He grabbed his board mid-air, landed crisp, and shredded a curving line in the snow in front of Zoey. Seeing what he meant, she made her turns opposed to his, so they created a series of loops when she closed his curves with hers. A design that belonged to just the two of them, at the top of a mountain.

He wanted to shout to Luke, "*Look at this. I get her. I know what she likes. Where are you? Showing off, instead of showing her a good time.*"

Instead, he did a series of surface turns with his board. She clapped, egging him on. They swerved through trees, waving at each other through the branches, and when they came out and hit the drop, he crouched low, letting the speed take over, until he felt like he was barely skimming the earth. Gravity had no hold on him, and maybe, just maybe, anything was possible.

Chapter Twelve

ZOEY

Watching Parker fly down the mountainside never got old. While Luke moved with purpose—a bulldozer looking to blast his way *through*—Parker and his board seemed like one entity. He made snowboarding seem reverent, a thing of purity and grace. It was beautiful. Like a bird in flight.

Zoey snorted. That was a little whimsical of her, but she couldn't help herself. He looked back to check on her and smiled, this warm, happy, thoroughly Parker smile that made her knees weak from the sheer freedom of it.

Wherever the feeling came from, this wasn't the best time for it. She lost her balance, landing on her butt and sliding to the edge of the trail. Thank God they'd passed the steep part, or she would've careened nonstop until a tree caught her…

…or nothing but air did.

She shivered and pushed herself upright. Parker had come to a halt and was unbuckling his bindings, probably so he could climb up to her.

"I'm fine," she called, waving him on. "Just, uh, a little spill."

She'd had worse, but staring as her best friend shredded a trail as the reason? Unheard of. She didn't lose her concentration like that even when she was admiring Luke's athleticism.

God, was steam coming off her cheeks? It had to be—they were on fire and it was well below freezing up here. This was so embarrassing.

Parker was climbing up toward her anyway, which made her more flustered. He was always so overprotective, but in a good way. "You okay?" He looked her up and down—purely clinical, making sure she wasn't broken somehow—but she flushed hot all over anyway.

Yep, she was definitely broken…it just wasn't in a way he could see. Besides, recognizing her best friend was pretty damn gorgeous on his board wasn't that big a deal, right? She was simply appreciating nature's work.

Right?

Her heart fluttered an uneven beat when he brushed snow off her back…and her *backside*. All with a sweet frown of concentration, and nothing else behind it. He was worried, that's all. Because there was no way they were anything but friends. Like Luke with the sleigh ride, if she told Parker she thought he was cute, he'd double over laughing.

Okay, maybe he wouldn't laugh—he'd get that same tired expression *she* always did when someone commented on her looks. The gene pool had been kind to both of them, but that wasn't who they were. He understood that better than anyone. Luke used his looks to make things happen, and that was fine, smoke 'em if you got 'em. But Parker? He knew it hurt to be dismissed because you were "pretty."

Which was why she'd never tell him. Their friendship meant too much to her.

"Zoey? Does anything hurt?"

My heart? My head? "Just my ego. Sorry. My legs must be a little less conditioned than I thought."

"It's icy up here." And that's all he said about it. No teasing. Simple kindness, nothing more.

They started down the trail again, but Zoey couldn't shake the feeling something was about to change…and maybe not for the best.

"I dare you to sing 'Sleigh Ride' while we're on the sleigh." Parker handed her a Styrofoam cup. "Double dog dare you."

"Dude, you have no idea what you're asking." She wrapped her hands around her hot chocolate and blew on it. The steam warmed her numb face. "I have the worst voice anywhere."

"I know," he said. "That's why I dared you."

"You're a mess." They went to stand in line for the sleigh and she hugged her arms to her chest. "I wonder where Luke is tonight. He doesn't know what he's missing."

She swept a hand around the staging area where the sleighs pulled in and out. White Christmas lights were strung on poles, twinkling down on the snow, which turned a twilight blue. Overhead, stars shone in a black sky, clear and sharp in the cold. In Colorado, she always felt like the stars were in reach.

Parker rubbed his chin. "I'm not sure where he is. Probably moonlighting as an elf at Santa's cottage downtown."

She grinned. "I might pay to see that."

"I might pay to see that, too. The thought of my brother in pointed shoes with bells on them? Priceless."

She laughed and squeezed his arm. "That's not right. Not even a little."

"I'm so wrong, I'm right."

"A case could be made." Zoey drifted closer to him. The air was frigid tonight, probably low twenties, and she'd hunched down inside her coat. Feeling bold, she nudged her way under his arm, and he pulled her against his side. Instant comfort, like always...so why did her pulse jump?

"Am I your space heater?" he asked.

His voice had gone low and husky and she shivered a little. His cheek brushed hers—accidentally?—and the roughness of the stubble on his jaw made her shiver again.

A case could be made for all kinds of "not right" tonight. The sleigh ride was starting to sound like a stupid idea for real, just not for the reasons she would've guessed.

"Maybe." She managed a normal voice, somehow. "Perks of being my best friend."

"Uh huh." Did he sound disappointed? Or was she *hoping* she heard disappointment? What was going on with her?

The line slowly shortened as sleigh after sleigh pulled away. Finally, only the family in front of them remained. The ticket taker had already put a chain on the gate behind them. No going back now—they'd made the last ride of the night. The sleigh pulled up, a massive thing drawn by four enormous horses. An attendant opened the gate to let them through.

The driver called, "Uh, Jamie, can you count, son?"

"Huh?" the attendant answered. "There's six."

"And the sleigh holds five. Two on the front bench, three in back."

Zoey's stomach sank. They couldn't all fit. "And this is the last ride of the night?"

"Yes," the disgruntled helper said.

The family had already hopped into the sleigh. The mom caught her eye, gave her a knowing smile, and told the kids to come sit in the back. "My little one can ride on my lap."

Zoey shot her a wordless look of gratitude, but Parker

upped the ante. "Or Zoey could ride on mine."

Her heart shot into her throat. His expression was perfectly calm, like it was no big deal…and it wasn't. She sat on his lap all the time, usually before wrestling him for the last package of Skittles. Tonight the thought made her chest ache, and not unpleasantly.

The mom in the back of the sleigh had to look away, but Zoey caught the smile behind the fingers pressed to the woman's mouth. The older child, a girl about eight, took that to mean she could sit up front again. She hopped out of the sleigh and back into the front seat.

"I don't mind sharing," she declared. "If you don't mind sitting in a boy's lap." She lowered her voice and put a hand to her mouth like she was telling a secret. "Hopefully he doesn't have cooties."

The mom's shoulders shook with laughter, and Parker laughed, too. "I'm cootie-free, thank you very much." He looked back at Zoey, a dare in his eyes. "Will the horses mind another person?"

"Aw, tiny thing like her? They won't even notice," the driver said. "You'll have to hang on tight, but it's all right by me."

Parker climbed into the sleigh and held out his arms. Wondering what the hell she was doing, Zoey slipped onto his lap and settled herself. His arms came around her at once, and the driver whistled at the horses. The sleigh started with a lurch, pressing her against Parker's chest.

Breathe. In and out. Just breathe.

His hand roamed up her back. "You comfortable?"

She held very still. "I'm fine. You're keeping me nice and warm."

Which was true. In fact, he was keeping her a little *too* warm.

He's your best friend.

I know.

So, don't let this go too far, idiot. Remember, you have the hots for Luke, so don't confuse things.

But, but…

No, buts. It will ruin everything. *Slow it down.*

Tell that to her pulse, which raced ahead of her good sense.

The horses plodded through the snow, pulling the sleigh like it weighed nothing. The breeze had quieted, adding to the hush that only the horses' bridle bells broke.

Parker's hand slid up her back. She could feel its warmth through her coat, which made her shiver again.

"You cold?" he whispered.

She shook her head. His face was so close…his *lips* were so close. If the sleigh hit a bump, they'd collide in a firm kiss. Which wasn't the worst thought she'd ever had…

God, what she was doing? He was her *friend*, and there were rules, boundaries. She knew all this, and understood the perils of having a guy best friend. You had to stay neutral, one of the boys, or things went topsy-turvy fast.

So what had she done? Volunteered to ride sitting in his lap. Self-control, thou art worthless.

She leaned against him while her thoughts tumbled about in her head. She was warm, cozy, and held tight by a boy she'd trust with her life. At home, she never felt like this. She always had to be on her guard, always the one people watched and looked to for cues. Here she could let all that go and enjoy a silly sleigh ride, even though most of her so-called friends at Alderwood would declare it a lame way to spend an evening.

And yet, she wasn't sure she should be letting it happen. She wasn't even sure *why* it was happening.

"Enjoying this?"

Parker's whisper tickled her ear, sending an ache through her belly. She turned slightly to find his lips an inch from hers again. She didn't want to hurt him, or lead him on. But, right now, he was looking at her in a way she couldn't decipher. Something that made her want to cling to him and explore his mouth with hers.

What was *wrong* with her?

"I was thinking," he whispered, "that maybe I should kiss you."

She could only goggle at him…had he read her mind? She needed to stop, think, but her body didn't care for that idea, and she didn't move away. "You were?"

"Yes, but only if you want me to." The corner of his mouth turned up and her eyes followed the movement. "Do you?"

Her pulse had already kicked up ten or a hundred beats a minute…but the fact that he *asked.* Most guys forgot that part. They just swooped in, and you either had to dodge or endure. "I…I don't know."

He smiled and reached up to cup her cheek. "Fair enough. Just stop me whenever."

They leaned toward each other and Zoey let her eyes flutter shut…right as the sleigh hit an icy patch, jolting everyone. Her eyes flew open just in time for Parker's nose to ram into her cheek. She yelped, and the mom in the backseat let out a little huff of disappointment.

Oh, Lord, they'd been in-sleigh entertainment, and she hadn't even noticed.

"You okay?" Parker's expression made her think of someone surfacing from deep water. His blinks were too slow, his breaths too fast.

"Yeah."

The sleigh came to a halt. "We're back," the driver said. "Thank y'all for coming out."

The family climbed out of the sleigh, the mom murmuring something like, "Darn it. I thought they—"

The eight-year-old tugged Zoey's sleeve, frowning. "You

know, there are rules about keeping your hands to yourself in public."

"Marnie!" her mom said, looking mortified at Zoey. "Sorry. She's a little bossy these days."

She took the little girl by the hand and marched her away. Zoey looked at Parker, and they both cracked up. "We're bad influences."

He touched his nose to hers. "Looks like it. I'm kind of proud of us."

Zoey disentangled herself from him and climbed out of the sleigh. Parker didn't let her stand alone for long, though, and he kept a hand on her back the whole way to his Land Rover. During the ride home, neither of them spoke. There was something sacred and full about their silence. She didn't want to break whatever spell had been cast around them, even if she knew she'd pay for it later. This was the kind of thing that killed friendships, but she couldn't tell herself to stop letting it happen.

They pulled up to her house. All the lights were on next door, a warm yellow glow spilling through the glass onto the snow. The windows at her place were dark. The parents must still be playing bridge. "So," she said, suddenly nervous about spending time alone with Parker. Each decision she made from here on out had to be perfect, or she might ruin everything between them, and she couldn't bear it if she lost him. "What now?"

Parker took her hand. "Follow me."

Wondering what he was up to, she let him lead her into her backyard. A quarter-acre of unbroken snow glistened like a thousand tiny sparklers in the moonlight. His smile was sweet and boyish as he walked to the middle of the yard, then flopped down on his back to make a snow angel.

Laughing, Zoey hurried to join him. The snow soaked through her jeans and her cap but the stars were so beautiful overhead, a whirling infinity she wanted to capture, that it was worth damp clothes. At some point, Parker's hand touched hers, and she stopped working on her angel.

"Now the angels are holding hands," he said.

"Like they should be," she murmured. "You really are my best friend."

He stood, then pulled her up so that she faced him. "You're my best friend, too. But…what if…"

She held very still half-hoping, half-fearing what he had to say. "What if what?"

He gave her a wry smile. "Never mind. You're shaking—we need to get inside so you can warm up."

She let him take her inside, but she couldn't help feeling disappointed—and maybe a little relieved—that he never finished that sentence.

Chapter Thirteen

PARKER

Too many near misses tonight. Parker had almost blurted out how he wanted to be more than friends, and for a second, Zoey had looked interested in what he had to say. Then he saw that tiny spark of fear in her eyes, and decided to back off. He had time. The way she'd melted against him in the sleigh gave him hope.

So he had time.

He trudged through the snow. He knew he was doing the right thing, but what if he was misreading her cues? Losing her friendship would be the worst, so maybe he should suck it up and pretend nothing was happening. But his heart felt like it would explode soon, and what then?

No, the risk was worth it, knowing she fit against his side like they were made for each other. And they'd almost kissed. He was sure she wouldn't have stopped him, if the sleigh hadn't bounced them around.

The thought of her face so close to his sent shudders

down his spine. Yeah, the risk was worth it. He also probably needed a five-mile run to cool off his overheated nerves.

He went in the front door and ran into Zoey's parents putting on their coats. His mom asked, "You're back already?"

"Yeah, we went for a sleigh ride, then watched some TV. Nothing special." Nothing he'd admit to anyway. "'Night."

Their voices faded as he climbed the stairs. Maybe a good night's sleep would give him time to think of ways to make this right. And if it didn't, he'd keep trying.

By the time he got in bed, the house had quieted down, but the window across from his next door was still lit. That was Zoey's room. Knowing she was still awake made it hard for him to settle down. What was she thinking about? Him? Them?   ·

Or was she thinking about Luke? Had his brother made any moves? His moody bullshit on the mountain today made it seem like he hadn't, but Zoey had still asked about him, so he wasn't out of her mind completely.

Which sucked. He had to find a way to obliterate her interest in his brother, and soon.

Parker punched his pillow and rolled over so he wouldn't have to see her bedroom light anymore.

By the time he woke up—with a headache, no less—the sun cut a blinding beam across his bedroom floor. Groaning, Parker checked the clock.

Ten-thirty.

Crap, he was supposed to take Zoey to the terrain park this morning. He launched himself from bed, landing with a thud in his bare feet that earned a yelled, "Is there an elephant upstairs?" from Mom in the kitchen.

He flung open his door. "Sorry. Just realized I'm late."

A two-minute shower would be enough, right? He checked his phone. Huh, no texts. Patience wasn't Zoey's strong suit, but maybe she'd needed a sleep-in day, too.

Or maybe she was ignoring him. Could she have woken up this morning, wondering what the hell happened last night? Regretting it?

A cold weight settled in his stomach. What if she *did* regret it? Funny things happened when two people sat together under a starry sky. Maybe she was chalking it up as crazy hormones, or as a moment gone too far.

He could see her: *It was the moon, Parker. Full, you know? We're so close, this kind of slip was bound to happen. It didn't mean anything, right?*

And he'd smile, nod like he was relieved, then go home and punch the wall until his knuckles bled.

No. He wasn't going to give up, or let doubt take all this away from him. Today they were headed to his castle, a gauntlet made out of steel bars and sculpted snow. And that, more than anything else, would get her attention.

Nodding, he climbed into the shower. He'd make sure she understood last night was no slip, and certainly no offer for friends with benefits. He was in it for the long haul.

Once he had dressed and grabbed an apple on his way out, he ran over to Zoey's house. Luke was gone already, and had taken the Jeep. So much for sharing.

He knocked, bouncing on his toes. A butterfly swarm roamed his stomach at the thought of seeing her after last night. God, he had it bad.

Jen opened the door. She was dressed for a day of skiing, coffee mug in hand. "Parker? What are you doing here, honey?"

The butterflies in his stomach dropped out of the sky, dead. "What do you mean?"

"Luke and Zoey left more than two hours ago." She

frowned. "Luke said you'd meet them there."

Shocked, he could only shake his head. Luke had taken Zoey to Snowmass—without him. And she'd gone, after she'd scolded him for doing the same to Luke. She'd abandoned him, knowing full well it would hurt his feelings.

"You okay?" Jen asked gently.

"Yeah." He forced a polite smile. "Great. I forgot that was the plan today. I guess I overslept."

Her forehead wrinkled. "Are you sure that's all?"

No, not even close, but he wasn't going to vent to Zoey's mom on her doorstep. "It's fine, really. I'll…I'll head up there now."

And when he found Luke, there were going to be fireworks on the mountain.

Chapter Fourteen

Zoey skidded to a stop at the bottom of her second run of the day. Luke was leaning on his board, watching her. His smile was possessive, but his gaze was remote, like he was watching her, but seeing something else.

She pulled off her board and walked over to him. When he'd shown up at her door, looking gorgeous and dangerous, and asked her to come with him, she'd been thrilled, but uncertain about an offer out of the blue like this.

"What about Parker?" she'd asked, remembering how bad she'd felt when they left Luke behind, and wondering if it was some kind of payback.

"Sleeping in, getting extra beauty sleep. He needs it." Luke had flashed her a grin. "He'll meet us up there later. Besides, I seem to remember a girl who said I needed to spend more time with her."

Her heart had pounded at the way he leaned closer to her, something about that sway of his body promising more than he said. Enthralled, she'd caught herself nodding before she'd had time to question the arrangement. Instead, she'd gone to get her gear with her face on fire and her belly in excited, confused knots. She'd even taken a second to put on some mascara and lip gloss, embarrassed to be caught in a raggedy bun and no makeup.

Now, they'd come down a few blues, "warming up" as Luke said. For what, he hadn't explained, yet. "Are we going to the terrain park now?"

He shrugged. "Or we could go back up to Headwall. Parker hogged your attention yesterday afternoon."

Zoey flushed clear down to her toes. "So you want me for yourself?"

He slid an arm around her shoulders. "What guy wouldn't?"

The flush faded and Zoey went cold. That was the problem—every guy thought they wanted her for himself, without knowing what he was really getting in return. Like she was a prize. Luke knew her better than some, but not really enough to make his comment any less concerning.

She stepped out from under his arm and leveled a stare his way. "I'm not interested in all the guys. A good one will do."

"That so?" He smiled. "You're a long haul type girl?"

"I am," she murmured, looking away. Was he offering? And if he was, could she trust him to stick around? She knew he had a reputation as a charmer, always on the prowl for the next girl and the next, but she'd hoped she could change him.

Could she?

No, she wouldn't think about that. She had to believe she could, or the two years she spent waiting for this moment were wasted.

"How about some coffee?" Luke asked, checking his watch. "Maybe a quick bite? It's eleven already."

They went to Two Creeks and, like usual, a small group of

girls watched every move he made, whispering, smiling slyly, and giving Zoey "hands off, he's mine" looks.

"Your fan club is here. Again." Much as she wanted to enjoy Luke's company, he *was* a package deal, and that would never change. As long as *he* changed, she'd learn to ignore it. Probably.

He smiled and winked at the girls in the corner, and led Zoey to a table across the café. "Does that bother you? The fan club?"

It sounded like a challenge, especially after yesterday. "No." She met his eyes and held them. "They're temporary."

Luke's eyebrows shot up. "You know the score, huh?" With a somewhat bemused tone, he added, "Seems to be that way most of the time."

Zoey latched onto the opening. "Why? Why haven't you tried to settle down with one girl?"

He reached for her hand and ran his thumb along her wrist. Zoey froze, like a rabbit caught in the stare of a coyote. "I haven't found the right one, yet. I've had to test drive a few."

"More like lots," she squeaked out.

He laughed. "Yeah, you got me. But I'd only need one, right?"

He was still stroking her wrist, and it was hypnotic. His cocky façade faded, leaving only the Luke she remembered from her childhood. The fearless, wild, present kid she'd loved, and in a way, still did.

"Yes, only one." Her head felt muddled, like she'd had a shot of Jack. Her chest burned like she'd had a shot, too. It was too warm in here. She needed some air, but she couldn't look away from him. He had her in his grasp, and she didn't know if she could—or wanted to—pull away. Was this the moment? Would he finally see that she was more than enough girl for him?

He leaned forward, and it seemed like he was about to

admit something, when a sharp, "There you are!" interrupted them.

Zoey yanked her hand free from Luke's and stared up at a very, *very* angry Parker. "Oh, hello."

This wasn't how she imagined he'd be when she saw him again after the craziness at the sleigh ride. She expected awkward, maybe confused, sweet. Not teeth-gritting, fist-clenching pissed. She should've listened to her gut this morning, but she didn't, and now look where she'd landed.

"It's about time," Luke declared. "We thought you'd never wake up."

Luke's voice was too loud, somewhat fake, and Zoey's stomach clenched. Oh, no…how could she have been so stupid? She'd been so bedazzled by Luke's smile and willing to believe anything he said that she'd fallen right into the trap.

"You. Left. Me." Parker turned his glare on Zoey. "Did you honestly fall for that?"

Shame burned in her belly. "I, uh…"

"You know what, never mind. I need to practice for the contest." He turned toward the door, but gave her a withering look over his shoulder. "You two have fun."

Then he stalked out of the restaurant, and Zoey burst into tears.

"Oh, Zoey." Luke sounded genuinely sad. "I was only trying to show him that we're not going to wait on him if he won't set an alarm."

She doubted that was the real reason—Luke loved one-upping Parker—but whatever was going on with them had gone too far. She dabbed at her cheeks with her napkin, getting angrier by the second. The only thing she hated more than crying, was crying in public. "Well, you sure taught him a lesson. And you taught me one, too, about trusting everything you say."

"Yeah." He scratched his neck, face pink. "Sorry about

that."

She didn't have a chance to grill him about what had started the raging competition between him and Parker, because three college girls strolled over, eyes focused on Luke.

"You're Luke Madison," said a girl with a blue streak running through her ash-blond hair.

"Maybe," Luke said, turning on the charm as easily as breathing.

The blue-haired girl nodded to her friends. "Told you. I saw him race at Keystone last year." She turned back to Luke. "When are you going pro? You're a boardercross monster."

"Thanks." Luke smiled his killer smile. "Why don't you join us?"

Blue hair gave Zoey an appraising look. "Is there room?"

Zoey couldn't believe it. Here he was, reeling them in, one-by-one, all while sitting next to a girl he'd made cry. Fury built in her chest like steam in the espresso machine behind the bar. She'd have to vent it soon, or she was going to blow.

"We could pull up a chair or two," Luke said, giving the girl the same lazy smile he'd used on her earlier.

Zoey seethed—she was done here. "You know what, I was just leaving."

As soon as she was out of the way, the blue-haired girl jumped into her seat without a thank you, chatting Luke up as if Zoey didn't even exist.

She stalked outside, hugging herself. Her jaw was gritted tight, and her breath came out in furious puffs of steam. Why did Luke enjoy girls hanging all over him, with a new girlfriend every weekend? At the table she'd thought maybe he was starting to understand he couldn't live that way long-term. His smile might be catnip to every girl—her included—but unless he straightened up, he'd end up lonely.

You know what, though? Fixing him wasn't her job. And it might not ever be.

Chapter Fifteen

PARKER

Parker sat at the edge of the terrain park, head in his hands. What had he done back there? He was mad at *Luke*, not Zoey, but who did he yell at? The girl he loved more than anything. Testosterone sucked. So did bad judgement. He had an overabundance of both. Still, knowing she fell for Luke's trick *hurt*.

And what about the part where they'd been holding hands? That sight had made him want to break things.

"Hey, P-Mad!" a female voice called.

He looked up. Shawn Beldon waved madly, her boyish face split in a wide grin. She was with a group of guys he normally hung out with. They skated over and he stood to meet them. "Hey, Shawn. Guys."

The Guys—four of them, two named Tyler, one Max, and one Balthazar, whose dad was a hippie—nodded in unison. That's why he called them "The Guys." They were a single unit, and travelled in a pack. He was allowed to join them,

Shawn, too, but only as an outside addition.

"Practicing for tomorrow?" Shawn asked.

He looked across the park at all the familiar jibs and rails. A little flying would clear his head. He owed Zoey an apology, but anger still nipped at his veins, and he should work that off first. "Yeah. Let's do it."

Parker shook out his shoulders, and went to the starting gate. He tightened the strap on his helmet and closed his eyes a second to catch some Zen, rocking his board back and forth to get a good feel. Finally, when everything went still and quiet inside of him, he tipped his board over the edge and flew.

That's what it felt like—flying. He took the twenty-foot kicker first, launching himself into a backside 540 to whistles and catcalls from other boarders. He landed clean, and turned for the main course, not giving himself time to think. Moving would erase everything.

The first rail came up, a down-flat-down. Perfect. He jumped a small mogul and landed on the rail, pulling his board into a 50-50 before turning back and making a grab as he flew off the end. He stomped the landing and decided it was time for a show.

A box came up next. Parker sprang onto it, conserving his energy so he could do a 540 off the end. He barely had time to register the look of delight on Shawn's face before the end came up, then he was spinning and the world was a crazy top for a second. He stuck his landing, cutting an edge in the snow. This was his element. All fine-tuned perfection. A place where he could practice his patience and master a skill not too many had. Something his brother never quite learned to do.

Luke was going to be in for a surprise tomorrow.

The crowd at the bottom grew as Parker zig-zagged around a group and slid over a rail. Feeling cocky, he saluted The Guys when he flew off the end. Cheers erupted from the crowd.

The last advanced obstacle was another kicker—not quite as big as the first one, but still twelve feet. When he went airborne, he bent his legs up to grab his board, before landing and taking a hard cut on his toes to slow his board in a spray of snow.

Five feet away from Zoey.

His glee faded at the sight of her. Oh, man…what was she doing here? And had she been crying?

Shawn ran across the snow and flung her arms around him. "Are you not the baddest badass in all of Snowmass? Ha! That rhymed." She turned and saw Zoey. "Hi there!"

Zoey gave her a dark look that quickly focused on Parker. "Hello."

Shawn frowned. She was about the nicest person you'd ever meet. She was also gay. Parker toyed with the idea of letting Zoey think she was a groupie, but Shawn would probably punch him for it later. Her girlfriend was an Olympic hopeful for deadlift, on top of it. Between the two of them, he could end up damaged if he pulled that prank.

He stepped out of her arms. "Zoey this is Shawn."

"Oh, so this is Zoey?" Shawn replaced the frown with her quick smile. "Nice to meet ya." She shook Zoey's hand with the friendliness of a spaniel puppy. "Parker talks about you a lot. Guys! Come meet Zoey!"

Zoey's death-glare crumbled into outright bewilderment. "Your name is…Shawn?"

"Yep." She laughed. "Shawna, actually, but that's hardly a good board name, is it? Why not be Shawn after His Eminence?"

Zoey mouthed "His Eminence" and Parker choked back a laugh. "Shaun White."

"Uh uh, no taking his name in vain." Shawn wagged a finger in his face as The Guys trooped over. "Zoey, meet The Guys. Guys, Zoey."

They said, "Hello," more-or-less in unison. Breaking with tradition, Balthazar stepped forward and took her hand. He kissed it and murmured, "A pleasure to meet you, finally."

Zoey broke into a smile and Balthazar's ears turned red.

"These are my people," Parker told her, after giving Balthazar a good-natured shove back into the collective. "They'll compete tomorrow."

"But they won't win." Shawn whacked him on the back. "This guy will."

"Um, I forgot to tell you. Luke entered," he admitted to the crowd.

Shawn cackled. "How in the name of His Eminence did you talk him into that?"

"It's kind of hard to explain." He darted a look at Zoey. "I appealed to his ego some."

Zoey was watching the ping-pong of the conversation, her expression softening. She'd probably come here to chew him out for snapping at her—and he deserved it—but this unruly scrum of crazy snowboarders had an impact on her. She'd never seen this part of his life, despite the fact that all these people had obviously heard of her.

"So, uh, you want to watch us practice?" he asked, hopeful.

She gave them a slow nod. "I'll go you one better. I want you to *teach* me."

Shawn smacked her on the back. "You've got balls, Blondie. I like that in a girl. C'mon, let me show you around."

And to his great surprise, Zoey went with her.

Chapter Sixteen

Parker's friends spent the next few hours taking turns teaching Zoey each of their trademark skills. Most of it was too advanced, but they watered it down, and by the end, she could do a wobbling 50-50 on a low rail. When she landed with only a small slip, but didn't fall, they applauded her.

She flushed at the praise, pleased at her progress, and gave The Guys and Shawn hugs. "Good luck tomorrow. All of you."

"Aye, we'll need it," Shawn said, laughing. "P-Mad here, he was built to dominate. Should go pro."

Pro? She looked Parker over, who carefully avoided her gaze. He'd always told her this was just a hobby. What was going on here?

"But I won't." Parker scuffed at the snow with his boot. "I like doing this for me rather than a sponsor."

"Purity," one of the Tylers said. "Respect, man."

"But you're still going to try to smoke Big Man, right?"

Shawn asked. "This is your year. Say it and own it."

He rolled his eyes. "This is my year."

They must be talking about Luke, from the wickedness in Shawn's eyes. So there *was* a part of Snowmass that wasn't Luke Madison's playground. Zoey nodded to Parker. "You know, I was so busy taking my lessons I didn't see you practice. Would you run a few for me?"

Watching him out here had been an education so far. His confidence was so much higher, his presence larger, his dominance more certain. He was a whole different Parker, and she wanted to see more of him.

Shawn elbowed him in the ribs. "Come on…give the girl a show, eh?"

Parker ducked his head. "All right, all right."

While he jogged up to the top of the course, Shawn leaned in close to Zoey. "He's a special guy."

Zoey's stomach clenched. Was Shawn interested in Parker? The thought made her want to punch something. *God, possessive much?* "He is. He's been my best friend forever."

"Oh, we know." Shawn gave her a knowing smirk. "He told Mandy and me all about you last week before you came. He was excited to see you."

Shit, did Parker have *two* groupies? Or more? "Mandy?"

"My girlfriend." Shawn's forehead wrinkled. "Wait, are you not down with that?"

Zoey had burst into relieved laughter, then felt guilty for being relieved. "No, I'm totally fine with that. I just…"

"Naw, I get it." Shawn patted her arm. "Here he goes. He's magic."

Parker waved at them, then jumped onto the downhill. He took the first rail full speed, turning his board perpendicular to the jib. He came off easily, like he was stepping off a low curb, and zigzagged to the smallest kicker, about eight feet tall, and made a tail grab, before landing like he did this all day. He curved to the next jump, this one twice as tall, and spun off the edge, grabbing his board as his body whirled through the air.

Zoey's mouth hung open.

"You okay, there?" Shawn asked, looking like she was in on a secret. Her eyes gleamed, and one side of her mouth turned up. "To tell the truth, I get a little lightheaded watching him up there, too, and I don't go for guys."

Parker skidded to halt next to them, grinning. "How was it?"

"Phenomenal," Shawn said, giving him a fist bump. "You're ready."

"Zoey?" he asked. "What did you think?"

"Phenomenal." She swallowed hard, forcing herself to think, to breathe, to focus. He'd called it a *hobby*. Whittling was a hobby—what Parker was doing was *art*. She couldn't wrap her brain around this. "You're amazing, Park. I mean it."

"Thanks." He stared at his feet, but like Balthazar earlier, the tips of his ears turned pink, and it was adorable. Luke would've given her the "you know it, baby," smirk, and said something suggestive about his "talents." But Parker couldn't even bring himself to look at her when she praised him, like he was embarrassed by it.

"We better go," Zoey said. If she stayed here another minute, she'd forget all about her vow to step back and figure out why she was feeling so out of control. Right now it felt like the snow was melting at her feet. What else didn't she know about him? "You still need to shop, and we won't have time tomorrow."

"Shop?" Shawn wrinkled her nose. "People do that?"

Zoey let out a shaky laugh. "When they don't want to be disowned by their Moms on Christmas morning, sure."

"Ah, then yes, he needs to get to it." Shawn picked up her board. "See you tomorrow."

She headed back to the park, The Guys in tow. Zoey watched her go. "She's something else."

"She is." He touched her hand. "Zoey, about earlier…"

She turned away as tears welled up on her lashes again. Too. Much. Crying. Too much *feeling*, too. Her heart would split down the middle, it was so full. "Let's not talk about it. Luke was wrong to play a joke on you like that. I didn't know. If I did, I would've waited for you."

Parker watched the boarders running the course. Maybe he realized she didn't want him to see her cry. "It's fine. I'm sorry I was upset. I was mad at Luke, not you."

"I know." She shook off her frown, determined to keep things from getting weirder than they already were. "There's a boutique I want you to see. It has perfect stuff for your mom."

Okay, a truce then. "Perfect for a guy with…" He checked the banking app on his phone. "A hundred and fifty-nine dollars?"

"Do you need to get *everyone* a gift with that budget?"

"Just Mom and Dad. I'm giving Luke coal."

She laughed. "What about me?"

He paused, but admitted, "I already have your gift."

Oh.

Chapter Seventeen

PARKER

Was that a blush? Was she blushing? Yes, her cheeks were definitely pink, and she wouldn't look at him when he opened her car door. Good sign, right? He took a little breath before climbing into the Range Rover. He shouldn't get his hopes up. For all he knew, Zoey was simply relieved they were okay again.

But that blush…

They drove downtown in silence. Every topic he thought of starting sounded stupid in his head, which was weird, because they never had a problem finding things to talk about before, including epic bouts of *would you rather*: Would you rather French kiss your math teacher, or eat a live slug?

Slug won, every single time.

He couldn't help wondering if their friendship would survive this experiment—whether it evolved into something more between them, or she got together with Luke. Although, the fact that she left Two Creeks—and Luke, the bastard—to find him was encouraging for sure.

"Wait! Stop here." Zoey pointed at a little store with lots of floral print fabric in the window. "This is it."

"Are you sure?" Just looking at the script sign over the door made him feel like he had hives. "And do I really have to go in there, or can I just give you my card?"

"Wuss." She undid her seatbelt. "You're going in there."

He groaned and put the Land Rover in park. "If you ask me to hold your purse, I'm out."

"No purse holding, promise."

A little bell tinkled when they pushed the door open. And the smell… God, it was like someone had smashed a bottle of rose perfume in a grandma's closet. Even the floor was girly—a squishy lilac carpet that made him feel like he was tiptoeing. Just to retrieve his man card, he stomped on it with his boots until Zoey gave him the stink eye.

A tiny gray haired lady came out from the back of the shop. "Oh, my. Hello, dears. What can I help you with?" She winked at Parker and he twitched. "Something for the girlfriend, I suppose?"

"Ah, uh…no." God, how he wished he could say *yes* to that question. "Um, something for my mom?"

Damn it, that sounded like a question. Why did it sound like a question? This place was dissolving his brain.

"Oh, well." The shop lady's tone was somewhat disapproving, like she believed a) Zoey was his girlfriend and b) he'd forgotten to buy her a gift. Neither of which was true. Yet. "Yes, we have many lovely—"

"This," Zoey said firmly, holding up a soft wool scarf. It was pale beige with gold thread shot through it. "He wants this."

"Yeah," he said, kind of awed. How did she *do* that? Was shopping her super power? "It's perfect. Mom will love it."

She nodded. "Of course she will. She has impeccable

taste." With a somewhat superior glance at the shop lady, she added, "As do I."

Parker bit the inside of his cheek to keep from laughing as the shop lady rang up the gift, looking a little sour. Probably because Zoey picked out something on the first try, and it wasn't a gazillion dollar sale.

Once they escaped, he sucked in a big lungful of snow-chilled air and let his head drop back so he could stretch his neck.

"That bad, huh?" Zoey said.

Her eyes were sparkling—someone was having a good time torturing him with shopping. "Tell me we're going into an electronics or ski shop next?"

"That depends." She grinned. "Where do they sell coal?"

He laughed. "No idea. But Dad said something about wanting new earbuds to wear while he was skiing."

"Then let's go."

An hour later, they had the earbuds, along with a knit cap Zoey said would bring out Dad's eyes—he had no intention of explaining that to his father—and a snow-bunny calendar as a gag gift for Luke. As if he needed more snow bunnies in his life, but whatever.

The snow had started again when they went outside. The sidewalks were busy, but everyone was smiling and happy, and no one more than Zoey. The holidays brought out the best in people, especially her. He couldn't wait to give her the silver charm bracelet he'd bought for her back in August, after seeing her gush over Mom's last summer. He'd bought three charms for it, too: a snowboard, a graduation cap, and a little heart with their initials on it. Sappy? Hell, yes, but desperate times made for desperate guys. If she let him, he planned to keep buying her charms until the bracelet was full.

Which meant he'd need a reason to buy her a birthday and Christmas present for the next six or seven years. Optimism was his middle name.

"So we're opening gifts Christmas Eve, right?" she asked. "Because my parents are still all about family only on Christmas Day."

"Yeah. We're going on our morning run up to Snowmass, then we're doing gifts and playing games after dinner at our place." He made a face. "I told Mom no more charades after last year."

Zoey threw back her head, laughing. It didn't subside until she wiped tears from her cheeks. "Hey, it's not my fault I thought you were miming a porno instead of that rodeo movie."

Parker flushed and looked away. "It was supposed to be a bull ride."

She touched his arm. "It was some kind of ride."

Some kind of ride. *That* sounded like a porn title. And now all he could think about was skin, mainly hers. But there were a few things still standing in the way—namely his brother. "So what's going on with you and Luke? He was holding your hand earlier."

That wasn't against the rules of the agreement, right? Flat out asking? Because he really wanted to know.

"I'm not sure," she said.

Wondering if he was about to rip out his own heart and stomp on it, he asked, "Tell me about it."

Chapter Eighteen

ZOEY

Parker looked so serious, like he really wanted to know what she was thinking. He was probably the only person other than Paige who did. But how could she talk to him about this? Especially when her own heart was such a tangle?

I'm not sure, she'd said. And she meant it. Luke was definitely flirting, and maybe interested. That's why she was so pissed off at Two Creeks. She wasn't jealous exactly, but she'd felt *dismissed*. Like his interest in her could only hold so long before it caught on someone else—particularly a someone with double-Ds. But when he looked at her, she felt like the only girl in the room. Could she cure him of his relationship ADD, or would it be impossible?

They were walking down the snow-covered sidewalk toward Parker's car, and her feet felt heavy with each step. Nothing was going as planned this week. Luke was at best intrigued, but that was all so far, and she had no idea what she needed to do to really get through to him. Deep down, she feared he only saw her looks, despite knowing her forever… or maybe *because* he'd known her forever. Worse, the sight of Parker on his snowboard had set off fireworks in her brain, and she kept flashing back to their almost kiss in the sleigh. He was her best friend…but she was completely confused now.

Why couldn't this be easy?

Parker cleared his throat and she realized he'd been waiting for an answer. "It's probably nothing. You know how Luke is."

"I do."

On a whim, she stood on tiptoe and kissed Parker on the cheek. "Thank you."

His eyes were guarded, cautious. "For what?"

She smiled. "Being you."

"I *am* kind of awesome." His smile came slowly, but when it did, it took over his entire face. Did he have any idea how cute he was? Probably not, since his brother hogged the attention.

"Now, now, cocky is Luke's thing." She checked her watch. "Almost dinner time. You need to get a good night's sleep, too. Tomorrow's a big day."

"We'll see." He sounded doubtful, and the smile disappeared.

She started walking briskly toward the car. "No. It will be. You're good, Parker. It's time for you to take a big step out of Luke's shadow and win this thing. Show him, and everyone else, that there's more than one snowboarding king in the Madison household."

"Will you cheer for me?"

The question was soft, uncertain. "Loudly. And obnoxiously. I'll make up stupid cheers for you."

He nodded slowly. "Okay, then. This could work."

She squeezed his arm. "It will. I believe it."

That night, after dinner and a good long text with Paige, Zoey lay on her stomach, reading. Another thing she couldn't admit at school: she was addicted to romance novels—the sappier, the better. HEAs were the only way to go in life. So what if she hadn't figured out how to get there herself? She had to believe she would, because the alternative was depressing.

Still, she hadn't faced the force of her feelings from this afternoon, or last night. It was so much to process, and she didn't want to burden Parker with any questions until the competition was over. Especially since she wasn't entirely sure what she wanted: her best friend as more, or her longtime crush forever?

Luke was safe—she wouldn't be risking an amazing friendship searching for something that might not even be there. Did she take a risk for a potentially big reward? Or did she keep doing what she was doing by going after Luke, and keep her friendship intact? Because if she made a move and Parker freaked out, they'd never get past it. Never.

God, working this out was going to take a while.

The light in the window across the way went on. Parker was in his room. Zoey glanced up, then gulped.

Holy. Shit.

Parker had forgotten to close his blinds. And he was wearing a towel. *Only* a towel. Their houses were close enough together that she could see his hair was damp from a shower. So was…the rest of him. Oh, Jesus.

Her entire body flushed white-hot. No, no, she really shouldn't be gawking like this. It was invasion of privacy. Except—she'd seen him in swimsuits their entire lives, so what was the problem?

The problem was that the towel was coming off any second.

Her will power wasn't working all that well, though, especially after the last few days, and she didn't think she could look away if she tried. Her curiosity was way too strong right now.

The other problem was those abs. And his shoulders. God almighty—had he been lifting? He wasn't as solid as Luke, but everything was well defined. He'd gone from lean to shredded since July. Like, paid-to-model-underwear shredded. Her mind snagged on the way his biceps flexed when he reached for something on his dresser.

Parker looked up suddenly, meeting her wide-eyed stare. For a minute, neither of them moved, then he laughed, sauntered to the window, and put a hand on the towel.

Zoey's breath froze in her lungs. Oh, God, oh, God, he was going to take it off. She put a hand over her eyes, but spread her fingers apart so she could peek. Still laughing, Parker loosened the towel. It started sliding off, showing that spot on a guy's hip that made smart girls do stupid, stupid things…

Then the blinds snapped shut.

She fell on her bed, giggling, arms wrapped around her aching middle. He'd done a half-Magic Mike in her window. Seriously, all he needed was a cowboy hat and slinky music, and women would pay serious money for that kind of show. What kind of best friend did a strip-tease for you?

She sat up suddenly. That was a really good question.

What kind of best friend did that?

Did he…could he…?

He'd almost kissed her last night. Today, he'd chewed out his brother for taking her to Snowmass without him. He'd introduced her to his friends—friends who said they knew all about her.

This was adding up to something way too big for her to process on her own. Because if she was right, she had the answers she needed.

She fumbled for her phone. Parker hadn't texted her, presumably to let his actions speak for themselves. It was just as well—she needed her other best friend right now.

Z: *You there?*

P: *Yep. Making cookies with Ben's mom.*

Zoey sighed in appreciation. Ben's mother owned a small bakery and her cookies were divine. Like honest-to-God-blessed-by-angels good. *Save some for me?*

P: *We'll leave you a fresh batch as a welcome home... and a thanks for the key.*

Z: *Fair deal. Um, can we talk? Like, can I call?*

P: *Sure, give me a sec.*

Zoey went to close her own blinds, not sure she could look Parker in the eye for the next few hours, then paced until her phone rang.

"Zoey? You okay?"

Paige sounded worried, probably because she'd asked to talk live instead of texting. Zoey hadn't meant to scare her, but she did need her best friend's advice. "I'm...okay. But I need your help deciphering something."

"Like what?"

Zoey took a deep breath, and finally told Paige about her life in Aspen. She admitted that she loved it here, told her about the snowboarding and, most importantly, confessed her feelings about the boys next door.

Paige listened quietly for a while, finally interrupting with,

"So you were in love with the older brother, but now you think you have feelings for the younger one, too? Parker?"

It sounded so simple, the way Paige said it. And a little shallow. If Zoey hated anything, it was feeling shallow, since most people assumed she was. "I don't think what I feel for Luke is love, exactly. Puppy love, maybe. A severe crush. Hell, it might've been pure lust." She put her head in her hand. "Okay, okay, it was probably the last one."

Paige laughed. "I'm going to need pictures to figure this out, you know." After Zoey texted her a photo of both brothers on the mountain, Paige whistled. "Hot damn. I think I understand the dilemma here."

"I know, I know. But, Parker, though…he's my very best guy friend. I don't want to risk our friendship—I'd be devastated if it didn't work out and I lost that. Most of my best memories have been with him. We've been a team since we were toddlers. I didn't even see it coming. The feeling hit out of nowhere. We went on a sleigh ride, and I suddenly wanted him to kiss me. Maybe it was the setting, but I don't think it was, because I can't get him out of my mind. He's really fun to be with, too. And he takes care of me."

"That doesn't sound so awful to me." Paige's tone was suspicious. "Why did you call me in a panic?"

"Um…" Zoey rolled her eyes at how tongue-tied she was. She normally said exactly what she meant, even if she did filter her words a little at school. "Our bedrooms are directly across from each other…the windows, too. His light came on, and there he was, wearing nothing but a towel. I about died."

"But you didn't close your eyes, did you?" Paige asked with sly understanding. "You looked."

"I totally looked. And he, uh, caught me watching and pretended to take off the towel, then snapped the blinds closed. Girl, I was *gawking*, and I was so busted."

"Why does this sound familiar?" Paige started to laugh.

"Oh, yeah. I seem to remember Ben stripping off his shirt to wash a car to impress you."

"Hey!" Ben called, nearby. "I was trying to impress *you.*"

Paige giggled harder. "And he sure did."

Zoey snorted. "I remember thinking your jaw was going to fall off."

"Speaking of Ben, I'm pretty sure he wants to say hi. He's lurking."

"I'm waiting patiently," Ben said, closer now.

"Put him on," Zoey said.

"Hey, Zoey. What's up?" Ben asked.

Happiness oozed through the phone, almost more than she could handle, and a lump formed in her throat. "Not much. Snowboarding a little. Angsting over a guy."

"Really?" He sounded intrigued. "There's a guy out there who meets your high standards? That's a statistical improbability."

"You could probably use that as your math thesis—the statistical improbability of a guy meeting my standards." They laughed. "But, yeah. There is."

"Whoever he is, he sounds like a guy I need to meet. I'll give you back to Paige, now."

"I think he misses you," she said after a pause long enough for a quick kiss.

"Oh, maybe a little." A pang hit Zoey right above the heart. She missed them, too. "But I think his world's complete right there in his mom's kitchen."

Paige's blush was audible. "Probably so. I know mine is. But, enough about me. What are you going to do?"

"He has that contest tomorrow. They both do. I don't think I should distract him before then." Or Luke, for that matter. They're doing some pretty extreme tricks and jumping off ramps taller than my house. I don't want Parker breaking a leg because I dumped my feelings on him."

"What if he says something to you? About the window, or the sleigh ride?"

Zoey rubbed her temples. "I'll be honest."

"Good for you." Paige paused. "And, Zoey? Don't worry so much about what people think. Honestly, if the StuCo found out you snowboard, they'd love it. Beautiful, badass Zoey—that's what they'd say. Plus, you deserve a guy who thinks you're amazing on the inside, not just the outside. Because you are."

Tears welled up in Zoey's eyes. Damn it—that was *three times* today. Choked, she said, "I love you."

"I love you, too." Paige made a kissy noise over the phone. "Now, go land that man!"

Zoey laugh-cried, sure her nose was running, but she didn't care. "I'll do my best."

But which one? The safe one she might only have for a little while? Or the risky one who already knew how to make her dreams come true? She knew what her heart wanted, but her head had decided to make her work for it.

She set her phone on the nightstand and turned off the lamp, hazarding a look at her blinds. They were closed, making her feel raw and shy, unsure of what tomorrow would be.

A faint light seeped through her window—Parker was still awake.

She couldn't go on like this. She had to figure out where she stood with Parker, and with Luke, and she'd decide.

Tomorrow.

Chapter Nineteen

PARKER

Zoey's face. God, the look on her face was going to be seared into his brain forever. Parker bit back a grin. He'd put on some sweats and flopped on his bed to think over what just happened. He had *no* idea what made him decide to show off like that, but she really liked it. Even with the distance between the houses—which wasn't much—he watched her turn red, and her eyes were wide.

In that moment, right before he dropped the blinds, he could almost hear her thinking, "Has he been working out?"

Yes, Zoey. The answer is hell yes.

He smothered a laugh, unable to keep it in anymore. What was she thinking right now? Wondering where that towel went? He didn't think she was going to give him a hard time about it later. No, she'd probably act like it didn't happen. If she did, he'd play it cool, too.

But what if she said something? What if there was more to her pink cheeks than simple embarrassment? If this was the thing that tilted her attention his direction, he wasn't above using it. He'd fight dirty.

Maybe he should've left the blinds open, let her see all the goods.

Parker threw his head back and laughed, feeling better than he had in weeks.

Luke appeared in his bedroom doorway. "What's so funny?"

"Oh, nothing." He hadn't seen Luke since the blow up at Two Creeks, but his brother didn't seem all that bothered and Parker decided to let it go—he was in too good a mood to ruin it. "What's up?"

Luke crossed his arms and leaned against the doorjamb. "About tomorrow…you talked me into the competition to show off for Zoey, didn't you? Or, more like to show me up in front of her."

Parker put a hand over his heart. "Who me? Never."

"Uh huh."

"Okay, maybe a little."

"I thought so." Luke shook his head, his smile looking forced. "Did you apologize to her, yet? For being a dick at the café earlier?"

Parker stood slowly, leveling a cool glance at his brother. "Yes. And I'm sorry I busted up your lunch, but you were the dick who caused the problem by ditching me."

"I could say the same about you a few days ago." Luke sighed. "But, bro, all's fair in love and war."

Parker's fists clenched at his side. "I thought you said you weren't going to fight dirty."

Luke pushed off the doorjamb, wearing his cocky grin. "I said I wasn't going to fight *that* dirty. We'll leave at eight tomorrow. Set an alarm, sleepyhead."

"Ditto." Parker watched his brother retreat to his own room.

Tomorrow, Zoey wouldn't even remember Luke's name.

The next morning, as soon as they hit the kitchen for a quick bite before going to Snowmass, Dad clapped his hands together. "I have something for you two."

He pulled two bags out of a kitchen chair. They were from Dad's company store, and Parker caught his eagerly when Dad tossed it to him. "Thought you guys would like the latest for your show today."

Inside the bag was a brand new jacket, black with a green splatter pattern, and the company name down one sleeve in white. They were next year's design. "These haven't even gone on sale yet!"

Luke was nodding in appreciation. His was white with a red splatter, and black logo—almost mirror-imaged. He weighed the jacket in his hand. "It's light."

"But warm. They'll keep you comfortable all day. There are vents if you get hot." Dad smiled. "A couple of hats in there, too. Knock 'em dead today."

Parker had already stripped off his old coat and put the new one on. He always wore black pants, unlike most of the more colorful boarders at the terrain park, and the new coat fit like it had been made for him—and it probably had. "Thanks, Dad."

"Yeah, thanks," Luke said. "See you up there."

"Don't forget your helmets!" Mom called from the pantry.

Luke rolled his eyes. "Mom, half the guys up there won't be wearing them."

"And you'd risk brain damage like the rest of them?" She came out of the pantry and put her hands on her hips. "Go get a helmet."

"Fine, fine."

While Luke went in search of a helmet, Parker winked and held his up. Mom gave him a quick hug. "That's my boy."

Finally, they were allowed outside. "Where's Zoey?" Luke asked as they loaded their gear in the Jeep.

"She's coming up later with Mom and Dad." Parker patted down his pockets to make sure he'd transferred everything from his other jacket. Contest nerves always made him obsessive about his gear. "No sense standing around in the cold for the next few hours."

And it was cold. Nineteen degrees with a sharp wind out of the north. Mom had frowned up at the sky a few times during breakfast, making Parker wonder if they were in for weather. Mom had an uncanny knack for predicting a big snow. But, so far, the sky was mostly clear, a light, high blue that only showed up in the dead of winter.

They climbed into the Jeep and took off for Snowmass. Luke kept both hands on the wheel and didn't bother with the radio. He always got nervous before a competition, and he had more reason this time.

"You know," Parker said. "You don't have to do this. I was being a jackass, talking you into entering."

"Nah, I'll do it." He cleared his throat. "I ride jibs on occasion, and I've been known to jump. It'll be fun."

"Okay, but the next time you run a boardercross, I'll enter so you can show me up."

"No." Luke's voice was flat. "Boardercross is a bunch of knuckle-draggers looking to lay out somebody. Kid like you should do stuff with more finesse and leave the brawling to me."

That was the closest Parker's brother had come to a compliment for a while, and he stared. "Now you're scaring me. You hit your head or something?"

Luke laughed. "No, but I might today."

They turned into the resort, and Parker didn't have time

to ask any more questions. As soon as they hit the main concourse, Luke turned on the charm and the swagger, gathering girls to trail behind them like the Pied Piper.

A few tried to hang onto Parker, but he smiled and gave them a polite brush off, before plowing ahead to the registration table.

"Parker Madison?" The man working registration smiled. "I was hoping we'd see you today."

Parker didn't know him, but nodded. "Wouldn't miss it."

The man handed him his competition jersey and number. Now all he had to do was wait.

Chapter Twenty

ZOEY

"Would you stop pacing, honey?" Mom asked, passing Dad a coffee cup. "Come eat some brunch. Tina and Jason won't be here for another half-hour."

Zoey trudged to the table, sat, and picked at a cinnamon roll. She hadn't heard from Parker this morning, which probably didn't mean anything—he needed to focus on his competition. She understood, but waiting to talk to him was torture. She'd lain awake for hours thinking about the peek she'd had through the window, and now she kind of wanted to see even more.

Jesus.

What about Luke? They were still on to go dancing tonight, and she wasn't sure she wanted to until she figured out what she wanted with Parker. Should she cancel?

A wave of cold washed over her. God, she was going to ditch Luke for his brother. After all those months of pining, too. Luke had acted sort of interested, but never really committed. So maybe it wasn't really ditching him if nothing had happened in the first place. Besides, the more time she spent with him, the less she'd...

The less she'd enjoyed it.

Could she really have been so blind? Sure he was gorgeous—how ironic that she'd judged a book by its cover. He was a decent big brother. He was a great snowboarder. But more and more, she thought maybe that was all. A pretty face, always on the lookout for the next new thing. Something she never wanted to be.

Which left her a pretty outstanding, terrifying option: falling for her best friend. Who might, or might not, want her in return. She thought he probably felt the same way, but if she screwed this up, she could lose one of the best things in her life. One wrong assumption, and she ended up alone on NYE, wishing she never came to Aspen. So how did she figure this out? Parker *had* been flirting with her...which should make this easy. But what if he was just messing around, thinking they were playing a game?

And why the hell couldn't she just ask him and get it over with?

Because the argument's a circle, silly girl. To find out if Parker likes you, you have to ask. And if you ask and are wrong, things will get weird.

But aren't they weird already?

What if he *was* ready for something more? The very idea made her quiver inside, but was it nerves or eagerness? She needed time and space to understand it all.

The sight of him in the window flashed through her brain again...and now she needed air.

Zoey stood and paced again.

"It's hopeless." Dad gave Mom a wry smile before turning to Zoey. "They're going to be fine, chickadee. These boys were skiing by the time they were two, and have boarded all winter for years. Have a little faith."

That was the problem. She had faith in their skills. She just lacked faith about her own heart.

Zoey found a place in the spectator line along the track, just below the second set of rails, with a great view of the first and second jumps. Snowboarders, dressed in everything from skinny jeans to baggy skater pants, with jackets in every combination of every color, milled around, waiting on their turn to take the lift up. More than half of them wore only caps or hoodies without helmets. Hopefully there wouldn't be an eyeball incident today.

She shuddered. Taking a blue without a helmet was one thing. Flinging yourself into the air at forty miles an hour without headgear? Yeah, not the best idea.

"Zoey!" Shawn, dressed in bright blue ski gear, shoved her way through the crowd to stand next to her. "Ready for this?"

She nodded. "Why aren't you up there?"

Shawn waved a hand dismissively. "Won't let me compete with the fellas. I won the women's division this morning."

"Sweet!" Zoey give her a fist bump, laughing because she'd never do that with anyone at school. Too "dude-bro" for Zoey Miller, Class President. "Thinking about trying for the X-Games?"

"Aww, maybe in a year or two. We'll see." Shawn shrugged. "Now, who really needs to think X-Games is P-Mad. Dude defies gravity."

Zoey had to focus on the crowd on the other side of the course to hide her flushed cheeks. "Yeah, he looked pretty good yesterday."

Both on the course, and off.

"Nah, he was keeping it tight yesterday." Shawn waggled an eyebrow. "Today you'll see the freak-flag fly, my girl. He's the best kept secret on this whole damn mountain."

Zoey stared up to the starting gate at the top of the course, wondering why he'd never mentioned it to her. She knew he loved the terrain park, but until yesterday, she didn't know he was *that* good. She had to live through stories of every one of Luke's wins, but Parker didn't talk about it. "He's full of surprises these days."

Shawn barked out a laugh. It sounded like a seal, and the crowd around them chuckled—Zoey included. "Girl, you really have no idea. But you should know." Her expression went serious. "He's excellent. I don't think his own brother even knows how good he is. Luke's amazing and fearless on boardercross tracks, but he's a diva. This time, it's P-Mad's turn."

Zoey let out a slow breath, trying to ease a pang in her chest. Shawn was more right than she knew. "I think so, too. I think it's definitely Parker's turn."

"Ladies, gents, peeps of all flavors!" a boyish voice announced over the loudspeakers. "Are you ready to have your minds blown?"

The crowd cheered with reckless abandon, and Zoey cheered along with them. Yes, she was totally ready to have her mind blown—maybe even altered forever.

"Good to know, because here we go!" the announcer yelled cheerfully. "First up, Jack Boren, from Keystone, Colorado."

One by one, the boarders took their first run along the course. Some were pretty good. A few were excellent. And a lot were clearly amateurs looking for a chance to hit a forty-foot jump. There were some big wipe-outs, with one guy being carried off by paramedics. He gave the crowd a thumbs up, but by the time Luke's name was called, Zoey's palms were slick with sweat, and her stomach was about to revolt in protest.

"Oh, lookie here!" the announcer sounded like he was about to wet himself. "We got ourselves a ringer… boardercross legend, and Snowmass's own—Luke Madison!"

The crowd roared with approval, and Zoey leaned against Shawn, her knees having gone weak with nerves. Shawn patted her on the head. "He'll be fine."

Zoey held her breath when Luke appeared at the gate. The announcer's tone became all business when he said, "Luke Madison, number fifteen, dropping in."

Luke slid into place at the top of the course, and shook out his arms. He looked small from this distance…and he looked tense. He fiddled with his helmet, obviously uncomfortable, and took a deep breath before tipping over the edge.

His run started clean and he definitely looked more at home than the amateurs, but Zoey could see how tightly wound he was in the way he moved. He took the first set of rails fine, and landed well, but Shawn shook her head.

"What?"

"Meat and potatoes. Dude's gotta give us more style. Basic 50-50 won't get him into the top ten."

Luke had already made the second rail. It looked like he was shooting for the middle, more difficult ride, but swung out to the right and hit the shorter, flat rail, instead of the graduated one.

Shawn hissed with displeasure. "Come on, Luke. Don't take the girlfriend ride. That down-flat-down was fine."

Zoey had no idea what she meant, but even she could tell Luke was either phoning it in, or he was being really cautious.

When he hit the first jump, she got her answer—he went for the smaller ramp on the right, pulling a neat 360 with a grab, but his landing was messy. He stayed upright, and went for the middle ramp at the second jump. She expected him pull out the stops, but he did a 540, wobbling in the air, and came down hard.

The landing pulled his feet out from under him and he rolled several feet before stopping.

"No!" Zoey's heart shot into her throat and she stood on her tiptoes to see if he was okay. At least he'd worn a helmet today. A minute went by—feeling more like an hour—then he got up slowly, gave the crowd a wave and walked off the course.

She clasped her shaking hands in front of her. Why had Luke agreed to this contest? It was obvious he wasn't quite ready for it. Was it because Parker dared him, and his ego wouldn't let him quit? If so, he learned a painful lesson in taking the bait.

"Ouch." Shawn shook her head sadly. "He needs to stick to boardercross. Smaller moguls and pack fights are more his thing."

"I think he entered because Parker asked," Zoey said.

"That's some kind of brotherly love."

Zoey wrapped her arms around her middle. "It's some kind of something."

Three more boarders went, and Zoey was almost out of her mind by the time the announcer said, "Oh, boys and girls, get ready for this last competitor, because you're in for a show. Please welcome hometown slopestyle master, number eighteen, Parker Madison, from Aspen, Colorado."

And there he was, wearing a new black and green coat, goggles, and—thank God—a helmet. He looked loose, but focused—the exact opposite of how Luke looked. He looked *good.*

The crowd went crazy. Certifiably. Two girls down the line from Zoey blew him kisses, and all the boarders turned their attention up to the starting gate, expressions rapt. Even Luke, who wore a bewildered expression at his little brother's welcome at the starting gate.

"Is there something I should know?" Zoey asked, feeling dizzy. She wiped a shaking hand across her forehead. "Is he a rock star up here and he failed to tell me?"

Shawn gripped Zoey's arms, grinning. "Something like that."

The announcer came back on: "Parker Madison, dropping in."

Zoey held her breath. Parker slid back and forth a few times, then started down the course. Everything seemed to slow down as he approached the first rail. He took the jump onto the middle rail—the longest—twisted his board 50-50, sliding across without so much as a wobble. At the end, he rotated in the air, and landed facing opposite direction.

"Nice. 270, landing switch. That's good for points," Shawn said.

Zoey nodded. Her stomach was in knots, but her heart was on fire as Parker approached the second rail. Again, he took the more difficult ride, riding the down-flat-down rail like it was a nice little jaunt on a blue trail. He made a quick grab coming off and landed easily.

"Here we go!" Shawn yelled.

Zoey wrapped her arms around her middle. Not surprisingly, Parker was heading for the middle jump—the thirty-footer. Up he went, corkscrewing through the air like gravity was optional. She squeaked as he came down, but she shouldn't have worried. His knees jarred a little, but he was already on the move for the last jump.

"Backside double cork," Shawn said, eyes gleaming. "Pros do a triple. He's close to nailing that, too. Saw him almost hit one last week."

The crowd was screaming his name as he ran up the last ramp. Up, up, up he went, flying off the edge like a cannon ball, twisting his body before his board came off the hill. He grabbed the front of his board, and made two-and-a-half turns in the air, before landing farther down the back side than anyone else had, yet. It was a gorgeous trick, perfectly executed.

"Was that good?" Zoey whispered, her heart in her throat. "I think it was good, right?"

Parker skidded to a stop and threw his hands in the air. By the crowd's reaction, it had to be, and Shawn was jumping up and down. "Girl, that was a switch-backside-900. Hell *yes*, it was good!"

It was more than good. It was beautiful.

He was beautiful.

Zoey sucked in a sharp breath. When had it gone from his *skill* was beautiful, to the whole boy?

Her cheeks burned. That line she'd tried not to cross? She was standing on it. No, stomping on it in her favorite pair of cowboy boots. This was her best friend—falling for him shouldn't be on the menu. Except…it *was*.

Zoey let out a ragged breath. She felt the truth of it down to her core. Parker was beautiful, inside and out. She'd wondered if they were playing a game the night of the sleigh ride, that it might be something she could somehow take back, to convince her heart it was only the starlight talking. But now? Now, her chest was tight, and she had to clench her hands in front of her to keep them from shaking.

"Hey, something wrong?" Shawn asked.

"I…don't know."

This was too much, too big to process. Tears filled Zoey's eyes. She was so proud of Parker, but she kind of wanted to punch him a little, especially when the two girls down the line lifted their shirts to flash him. The weight on her heart had lifted, enough to make her jealous.

She let out a soft surprised laugh. Parker was a bigger deal on the mountain today that Luke ever could be. God… and she'd had no idea. On top of it, she was so relieved they both survived that her head started to hurt out of sheer stress.

"Final scores are in," the announcer said. "In third place, Jack Bowen, with an eight-five point two." After polite applause, he continued. "In second place, Balthazar Moore with eight-seven point six."

One of The Guys. The one who'd spoken to her first. That made Zoey smile. It was a shaky smile, but she was waiting on the last announcement.

"And, in first place…" The announcer laughed. "Oh, hell, you know who it is. Parker Madison, with a score of ninety-one point one."

The applause was deafening, and Parker waved at everyone. Luke had come out onto the course and flung an arm around his shoulders. Luke looked genuinely proud of his brother, and it hit her right in the heart. She took a couple of deep breaths, hoping to calm down a little and enjoy the show. Instead, she started shaking. She hadn't noticed the cold before, but now it was all she felt.

Shawn frowned. "You don't look so good."

"Overwhelmed, I think." She blinked back a few tears, and her head started to pound. Yeah, overwhelmed was a darn good word for it. "I was going to ride home with the boys, but I'm not feeling so hot. Could you take me?"

"Yeah, you bet." Shawn took her arm and waved to someone in the crowd. A tall, strongly built girl with a kind face forced her way through. "Mandy, this is one of P. Mad's friends. She's not feeling great, and I said we'd give her a lift."

Mandy looked Zoey over, then took her other arm. "Come on, sweetheart. You need to go home."

Zoey peeked over her shoulder toward the boys one last time, and they were both smiling.

So worth the trip.

Chapter Twenty-One

PARKER

To say this was the greatest moment of his life probably wasn't an overstatement. The cheers, the pats on the back, and the handshakes were great. But the best part was the proud, puffed up way Luke dragged him around the group, showing him off. He was truly excited about the win, even if Parker could tell Luke's ego hurt a little.

A guy in his thirties—a classic surfer/skater/snowboarder type with long hair and an expensive, well-worn board— stopped them.

"Brah, you're sick up there. My card." He held out a business card and Parker's eyebrows shot up—this guy didn't look like the type to carry those. He looked more likely to carry a joint. "I scope talent for an agent who books boarders for appearances and gets them into competitions. Even X-Games. Give me a call if you're interested in blowing minds for a living."

Parker took the card with the tips of his fingers. "Uh, yeah, thanks. I'll, um, think it over."

"Boss. Oh, and I can hook you up with the best coaches in the business, just sayin'.'"

The talent scout—or whatever you'd call him—nodded politely at Luke, then grabbed his gear and started for the lifts.

Luke plucked the card out of Parker's fingers and whistled. "Wait a minute. Mick Forester Agency—I know that name. He reps some of the guys I know. Kid, this is legit."

Parker shoved the card into the front pocket of his jacket. "I'll just file this under 'things I never saw coming' and call it a day."

"But don't you want to call them?" Luke raised an eyebrow. "This is a big deal."

He sighed. "I know it is, but I'm happy with my life the way it is. I want to study architecture and design ski resorts and snowboard parks for a living. Running the circuit is a hard way to go, and I'd risk getting hurt all the time. It's just not for me."

Luke shook his head, smiling. "That's so you. Humble to the end."

"Boarding is my Zen. I'm not interested in giving it up. Not really humility, but whatever." He paused, looking around. "Have you seen Zoey?"

Now that the nerves from the competition were over, he really wanted to see her. Her opinion on how his run went mattered to him a lot more than a shaggy-haired agent's rep. He felt like they were on the edge of their normal relationship, and it could tip either way. He meant to make it tip toward him… he just wasn't sure what else to do. He'd practically stripped for her, and had no idea what she thought about it.

Luke stood up tall and scanned the crowd. "I thought I spotted her earlier, but no. I don't see her."

Some of his joy evaporated. Was she upset with him? Had

he embarrassed her last night so much that she decided to stay home? God, had he read everything wrong?

His parents raced through the crowd to give them both hugs. "We're so proud of you, honey," Mom said, beaming. "You, too, Luke. You scared me to death with that fall, though."

"I was wearing a helmet just like my mother told me." Luke gave her a half smile. "Have either of you seen Zoey?"

"She came with us, but she left already." Dad pulled his phone out of his pocket. "She texted us to say she wasn't feeling well and went home. I think your friend Shawn took her, Parker."

He knew being disappointed was kind of selfish if she didn't feel well, but he wished she was here. He wanted her by his side for every best day, and every worst day. The problem was—he wasn't sure how to tell that. Or if he even could. Hell, she'd been holding Luke's hand yesterday, *after* she'd almost let him kiss her the night before that. That either meant his strong play was working, or she didn't have any idea what she wanted.

The awards ceremony started, and Parker took his spot on the first place podium, waving at the crowd. A couple of girls blew him kisses and gave him smiles usually reserved for Luke: "Come and get it, big boy."

He made sure to look elsewhere for the rest of ceremony.

As soon as he got home, he showered, intentionally leaving the blinds open again to see if Zoey was watching. Her blinds were closed.

Fine, then he'd take the party to her, so they could spend the afternoon figuring stuff out.

Mom looked up from her perch on the living room sofa

when he bounded downstairs. She'd already changed into yoga pants and a sweatshirt, her uniform for a long afternoon inside. "You going out?"

"I want to see if Miller's okay."

She laid her book on the arm of the sofa. "Good. I'm worried about her. Is something going on with you two?"

A hard seed of fear lodged in his throat. "I don't think so. Why would you think that?"

"She was really quiet on the way up to Snowmass." Mom bit back a suspicious looking smile. "Something had her bothered. Not sure *what*, though."

Oh, crap. Why had he goofed around last night? Why? He'd played his hand too far, and now she was upset, and...

"Parker, whatever you're thinking, she's not mad at you." Mom chuckled softly. "She seemed really eager to watch you compete. She had a lot on her mind, was all."

"She did?"

Mom didn't bother to hide her smile this time. She rose and put her hands on his shoulders. "She did. Question is, son, what are you going to do about it?"

He took a step back. "I don't know what you mean."

"Yes, you do." She settled back onto the sofa. "You won the competition today. Don't let that be the only thing you win instead of Luke." She hummed as she picked up her book and rifled through it. "Oh, look. Happy ending. I love those, don't you?"

For a second, he couldn't move. Couldn't *breathe*. What did she know? Had Zoey said something to her? "Yeah. Yeah, I do."

Mom started reading again. "See you at dinner."

Parker tumbled out the front door onto the slushy sidewalk, reeling like a truck had hit him head on. Was this it? Was this the chance he'd been looking for?

He hurried over to her house, slipping and sliding in his

rush. If anyone was watching, they'd likely scoff at the idea that he was today's slopestyle champ. *Dude can't even stand up on an icy sidewalk, how can he jump?*

The answer, my friend, is love makes you crazy.

Her parents' car was in the drive when he went to ring the bell, so he wasn't surprised when Jen answered. Like his mom, she was wearing yoga pants and a hoodie. Must be a dress code. "Is Zoey here? My mom said she wasn't feeling so well."

Jen glanced at the staircase behind her. "She's sleeping, Parker. Said she had a headache and wanted a nap before Luke took her dancing."

Before *Luke* took her dancing? "Oh. I'm going with them, too."

"Of course you are." Her mom's eyes twinkled. "I told her I'd wake her up in time to get ready. She said you were leaving at nine. See you then?"

"Yeah, sure." He turned to walk down to the driveway, his feet a dead weight. Zoey said Luke was taking her dancing? That was true, but he'd hoped…shit, it didn't matter what he hoped. What mattered was how hard he would work to make this night about the two of them, and *not* about his brother. He had to shake this off, hope that Zoey simply meant that Luke was *driving* her to the club. Because if she danced with Luke all night, he wasn't sure he'd be able to live with it.

"And Parker? I heard you won today," Jen called. "Congratulations!"

He managed a smile over his shoulder. "Thanks."

It was tempting to slump his shoulders on the walk back home, wallow a bit. But he wasn't going to. This was *his* day to shine, and he was going to damn well do it. Luke better watch his back.

Parker wasn't here to play.

Chapter Twenty-Two

ZOEY

"Honey?" A hand shook her shoulder. "Weren't you going out tonight? Shouldn't you be up?"

Zoey sat up, confused as to where she was. The grey afternoon light had turned dark, and the clock read seven. "Why is it so late? I only laid down for a second."

Mom frowned and snapped on the bedside lamp before pressing the back of her hand to Zoey's forehead. "You're burning up."

"I probably got hot sleeping. Too many covers." She struggled out of bed, putting a hand on the wall when the room lurched to the right. "The boys are coming over to take me dancing soon. A shower will sort me out."

Mom crossed her arms. "Maybe you should stay home."

"I'm fine. Really." She forced a smile, even though her temples throbbed in time to her heartbeat. That wouldn't stop her, though. She wasn't going to miss her chance to corner Parker alone, and up close, at the club. "I'll be down to eat in a bit."

Mom didn't look the least bit convinced, but she left Zoey alone. Okay, a few ibuprofen and a hot shower first, then she'd tackle a night at the club. She'd be fine. And if the room spun a little, that might be a bonus. If she got dizzy, she had an excuse to stumble into Parker without it looking weird. And totally natural for him to hold her up.

She checked her phone before heading to the bathroom. Two Snapchats from Luke, both pictures of him. Both telling her *how much* he was looking forward to going dancing with her. Zoey grimaced. This was going to be a complicated night.

She shivered when she climbed into the shower. The hot water made her feel cold instead of warm and the hairs on her arms stood up with goose bumps. Mom might be right, but it didn't matter. She needed to test her heart, and be sure she was ready to ask some tough questions about her relationship with Parker. Right now, she was sure, but she had to be doubly so.

What if he didn't feel the same way?

She sank down and sat in the bathtub, the hot water pounding her back, and wrapped her arms around her knees. If he didn't...it would break her heart. Could she still be friends with him? Probably, but could he be friends with her?

This was so confusing. Or maybe that was because she was seeing double. Groaning, she pulled herself upright and got out of the shower. It took two tries to plug in her hairdryer, but she wasn't going to let that—or the headache, or the new tickle at the back of her throat—stop her.

By the time the Madisons came over to play *Apples to Apples* with her parents, she was feeling better. She even ate a slice of pizza. She felt strangely full afterwards, even though she should've been starving after a long day without eating much. Now it was nice to sit by the fire, wrapped up in a hoodie and jeans, and listen to the silly combos the parents came up with. In twenty years, that could be her…with Parker.

Funny how a dream could change in a few days when you finally opened your eyes.

"Hey, anybody home?" Luke called, banging through her front door like he owned the place. Parker followed in behind. She stood to meet them, but stopped short. Oh, my God, they looked good. Luke had on dark jeans, a black button-down, and a wool jacket. He looked like a stockbroker out for a night in Manhattan. Parker hadn't done so badly, either, in jeans, a crisp white button down and a pair of brown leather boots she couldn't believe he even owned. Except they fit him…and were a little worn.

He'd even done something with his hair that didn't involve a ski cap. It was gelled into a gloriously perfect mess, and she nodded in appreciation, as a flush crept up her chest. "You two clean up nice."

"Always," Luke said, grinning. "We still going dancing, gorgeous?"

Behind him, Parker scowled. Zoey wished she could tell him not to worry, that she wasn't falling for Luke's obvious flirting, but all four parents were watching them with amusement. So she went for blasé, and shrugged. "If you still want to."

"Wouldn't miss it." Luke's eyes blazed with mischief. "Not to sound rude, though, but word around town is the bouncer's a real piece of work. Could you change into something that'll catch his attention?"

Parker's expression went from irritation to outrage. "She's not a Barbie doll, dumbass."

Luke held up his hands. "Hey, I'm asking her to wear something with flash, not a see-through dress."

"I don't approve of this plan, either," Dad said. "She'll wear a wool dress that covers her from shoulders to knees. And tights."

"Tights?" Zoey groaned, and her head started hurting again. "Dad…"

"Yes, tights, and a pair of those little shoes with the straps. The ones little girls wear?"

"Mary Janes?" Tina chuckled. "You want her to wear a wool dress and Mary Janes? To go dancing at a nightclub?"

Dad nodded emphatically. "Yes. Or maybe to a church social with lots of chaperones."

"Brian, don't be such a downer," Mom said, laughing. "She's eighteen, not seven."

"That's what I'm worried about."

Zoey sighed. "Will everyone please let *me* decide what I'm going to wear? Dad, don't worry. My outfit will end up somewhere in between convent and Beyoncé."

Dad pretended to consider. "Okay, but it better be closer to convent than Beyoncé. I've seen some of things she wears."

She ran upstairs to get dressed before Dad could demand that she wear a dress with a sash and ribbons in her hair. When she'd packed for the trip, she'd thrown in a red lacy dress she'd bought on sale that covered less than she was used to, thinking to impress Luke. It sounded so desperate now, and there was no way she'd wear it. There's no way Dad would let her wear it, either, even if he was teasing earlier.

She paused and ran a hand over the red dress. She'd gone so far to get Luke's attention: sexy dresses and makeup on the mountain, flirting and flattering. She'd let herself become a groupie, and realizing it stung. Not anymore—that wasn't the person she wanted to be. Zoey let go of the red dress, watching it slip between her other clothes. If she chose to glam it up, it would be because *she* wanted to, and not to impress anyone else.

She surveyed her closet. There was a silver miniskirt and black wrap top, which was elegant and made her look older. It was nice enough for a club, and she felt good in that outfit.

So what if it didn't have the "flash" Luke was looking for? It was the right thing for tonight, and she imagined Parker would probably appreciate it just fine. His opinion was what mattered now.

She took her time getting ready, and by the time nine rolled around, she was bundled up in her wool coat with the faux-fur collar partly because of the snow, and partly to make her dad wonder what she was wearing, just for fun. He eyed the black booties with the four inch heels with plenty of suspicion, but waved her on as soon as Parker opened front door.

"I know where you two gentlemen live," he said in a passably threating tone. "Back by one-thirty, or I'm rounding up a posse of gun club enthusiasts."

"Noted, sir." Parker expression was torn between amusement and terror, and Zoey's heart beat a little faster. He wouldn't look like that if he had nothing but good, clean fun on his mind, would he? Maybe there was hope after all.

"Come on, let's go before he threatens me with a girls-only Catholic school," Zoey said, pushing him out the door.

His hand settled at the small of her back. "You warm enough?"

It was a sweet thing to ask, especially since she'd foregone tights to spite her father. "No, but I'll live."

They hurried down the walk to Luke's car. The cold wind cut through her and the streetlights had strange halos around them, but when she blinked, they disappeared. Nothing to worry about. Must be her contacts…and not the start of bird flu.

"Here." Parker opened the door, then half lifted her into the Jeep's back seat before sliding in next to her. "Good?"

She caught Luke's eyes on them in the rearview mirror, something slightly mocking in his gaze. She turned away and leaned into Parker. "Better now."

His eyebrow twitched slightly, but he didn't say anything. "We're ready, Jeeves. Drive on."

"I should've sold you to the circus when you were four," Luke said. "Would've made my life easier."

They drove downtown slowly. Or maybe it seemed slow because the boys were ignoring each other, and it felt like the temperature of the car dropped ten degrees. She shivered, holding herself tight to stay warm.

"You sure you're okay?" Parker's eyebrows were pinched with concern. "You don't look like you feel well."

"I'm fine." She waved a hand. A fever and a headache weren't going to ruin this for her. Paige had ordered her to "land that man" and this was phase one of her plan to do just that. She couldn't quit now.

"We can still go home." His arm tightened around her. "That wouldn't bother me at all. A quiet night in would be fine after all that went on today."

"Oh!" Zoey sat up, feeling wobbly. "I'm so sorry I wasn't there for the awards ceremony today. You looked amazing. Shawn stood with me and explained all the tricks. The crowd loved you."

Parker ducked his head. "Thanks. I had a blast."

"You tell her about the scout?" Luke asked.

His tone was neutral, but Parker stiffened. "No. I wasn't planning to, either, so thanks."

"Tell me what?" She peered into his face. "Something wrong?"

"No. I got a card from a scout who works for a promoter, that's all."

"That's all, he says." Luke laughed, and Zoey wasn't surprised to hear a note of jealousy in it. "The promoter works with X-Gamers. A little push, and the kid could hit the big-time circuit."

"Can we not talk about this right now?" Parker rubbed

the back of his neck. "I'm not ready to think about it."

Zoey stared at the floorboards. The X-Games? The circuit? Would Parker forego college to snowboard for a living? And if he did, where would that leave her? No—she should be happy for him, not selfishly wishing he'd stick around. But…she couldn't bear the thought of him leaving. She closed her eyes, feeling sick, and she didn't think it was from the flu.

"Okay, fine. We're here, anyway," Luke said.

Here looked like an abandoned store front, with blacked out windows and a hand-painted sign over the door that read, "Edge."

"God," Parker said, "It looks like a cross between a totally cheesy youth club and a place to get ax murdered."

Based on the half-block long line of hot teens and twenty-somethings on the sidewalk outside, people clearly didn't share Parker's fear. Zoey chuckled. "If it sucks, we can go out for ice cream."

"Now, *that* sounds fun," Luke said.

"It does, Mr. Sarcasm." Zoey sighed. "And you're assuming we can even get into this place. There are fifty people waiting."

"Oh, I think we won't have any trouble." Luke flashed her a grin. "The bouncer takes one look at you, and we're in."

Zoey's stomach clenched, and Parker leaned over to whisper, "Don't listen to him. We get in, or we don't. Don't put yourself out there if you don't want to just because Luke said so."

"I won't," she murmured, thankful Parker understood.

Luke parked the Jeep and they hurried through the cold to get in line. A bouncer was walking down the sidewalk, eyeing people to let in. Once she got a good look at who was evaluating the potential clubbers, a little smile tugged at Zoey's face despite the cold. This was going to be more fun than she thought.

"You got any dynamite?" Luke asked, nudging her with his hip. "He's coming this way."

"Look closer." Zoey gave him a devilish smirk. "The bouncer's a woman."

"He has a shaved head."

"*She* has a shaved head." She nudged Luke in the hip like he'd done to her. "You got any dynamite, sweet thing?"

It was true—the bouncer was a tough, tall, bald woman with appraising eyes and the look of someone who knew exactly what she wanted. Luke's jaw dropped, but Parker winked and moved closer to the rope, pulling this sexy grin out of nowhere. Zoey's blinked, then blinked again. He looked so...so...hot.

The woman sauntered over. "You're the kid who won up at Snowmass today. Am I right?"

Parker didn't bat an eyelash. "Yes, ma'am. Here to celebrate."

Zoey's mouth stretched into a surprised—and gleeful—grin when the woman nodded. "How many?"

"Three," he said, pointing to her and Luke.

"Huh, you got yourself an entourage. Good for you." She stamped their hands with a purple "*E*" and nodded to the door. A protesting grumble started up from the rest of the line—all guys' voices. The girls seemed to understand exactly how they got in and didn't seem too peeved about it. More than one of them gave both the Madisons long looks as they moved inside. Zoey had to bite her lip to keep from laughing when Luke's shoulders rolled in a little.

How do you like a taste of your own medicine, buddy? Being ogled isn't so much fun, now is it?

The heavy sound of bass assaulted them as soon as they opened the door, then the smell of flat beer wafted out. A bored bouncer stood at the desk. "Stamps."

They showed their hands, paid the cover, then were

waved inside. The dance floor teemed with bodies, while lights strobed overhead in reds, blues, purples. Parker took her coat and waded into the fray to find a table. Luke stood at her elbow.

"Well? What do you think?"

She thought Parker's assessment was partly correct. A few people definitely looked like ax murderers, especially the skeevy group of older guys watching a drunk mob of girls dirty dance with each other.

But the half-teasing, half-mocking smile was back on Luke's face, and she was done with his baiting. She met his eye, not giving him an inch. "Looks hot. Think I'll go dance."

Feeling the eyes of every guy in the place crawl over her, Zoey found a half empty corner of the floor and started swaying with the music. Trying to forget all her confusion from earlier, she let the beat take over, and raised her arms over her head and danced like she didn't care. It felt good to let it all go, to remind herself this was her vacation. She'd get everything sorted out and it would be all better.

She hoped.

The room buzzed in her head, and she felt the music in her bones. The lights overhead did the halo thing like the streetlights, and the dancefloor was bathed in purple-pink. So beautiful. Sweat beaded on her forehead. Beautiful. The world was full of infinite possibilities, totally within her grasp. She let out a soft giggle, trying to drown out the ringing in her ears.

That feeling of freedom lasted all of a minute, then some drunk guy appeared in front of her like an unwelcome mirage. "Dance with me, baby."

He thrust his hips forward and attempted to grind against her. It took her a second to shake the cobwebs free, but she managed to cock a fist to knock his sorry ass out. Before she could swing, a hand clamped down hard on the guy's shoulder.

Luke stood behind him, looking like he was willing to commit a grievous act of murder. "She's with me."

The guy held up his hands and backed away. Zoey called after him, "And even if I wasn't, don't be a dickhead to the next girl you see alone!"

Luke laughed. "Did you want to fight that battle? Should I have waited?"

She waved a hand. "No. You saved me from breaking my fingers on his face."

They stared awkwardly at one another as a slow song started. People paired up all around them, and Zoey had no idea where Parker had disappeared to. Luke stood in front of her, but she really wanted Parker's arms around her, not Luke's. She looked all over the club, but couldn't see Parker over the people on the floor. The ringing in her ears had started up again, too.

"Want to dance?" Luke asked.

"Yeah," she said, giving up the search. He'd find her. He always did. She took a step toward Luke, scanning the dance floor one last time. The room spun and she ended up stumbling right into his arms.

"Whoa, there," he said, with a lazy smile.

"Sorry," she mumbled against his chest. Wrong arms, wrong chest, but it seemed like a good place to rest her head a second until the floor stopped moving. "Just tripped."

"Uh huh. Sure."

She was too tired to argue, and they moved in a slow circle, not paying attention to anyone else. "You know," Luke finally said. "I'm having a hard time with this."

She yawned and blinked to clear her vision before tilting her chin up to look at him. "What do you mean?"

"I've known you since you were in preschool, making mud-pies with my brother, but you've grown up," he said. "And here we are, dancing. You've grown into a beautiful, fearless woman, Zoey. I like what I see."

"You do?" Was he really making a play right now? Maybe she shouldn't have leaned against him. God, her head hurt. No…her teeth hurt. Wait—both her teeth and her head hurt, and so did her bones. What was he saying?

But Luke was laughing. "I wouldn't have said so if I didn't mean it."

His arms tightened around her, and he tucked her head under his chin. They kept turning, and the music was so loud. A little voice in the back of her head was reminding her there was somewhere else she wanted to be, but the rest of her was too tired to move.

"I was thinking," he murmured into her hair. "Maybe after this we can go out, just the two of us. There's a great lookout point not far from the house. You can see all of Aspen. It's gorgeous at night."

She swallowed. Her throat was so dry. "What?"

Luke laughed again. It rumbled in his chest and vibrated against her cheek. "I'm asking you out for a romantic drive. Sorry if I wasn't clear before."

"Oh."

"Just oh?" He sighed and turned them in a circle before adding. "I thought that might be what you wanted."

She pulled away and blinked up at him. "I'm not sure anymore. I…I don't know what's going on."

A brief look of disappointment crossed Luke's face, but he recovered with a smile. "With what?"

"With me." God, she was so tired. She waved a hand at him. "You. Parker."

"Parker." Luke's voice was flat. "Trouble in PB&J's universe?"

"Opposite," she mumbled. "Opposite of trouble."

"Zoey, what do you mean?"

Her head lolled against his chest. "I…what?"

"You okay?" he frowned down at her.

"I…don't know."

"In that case, maybe I should cut in." Parker appeared behind Luke. "I'll take it from here."

Luke released her and headed for the bar. Parker's jaw was clenched. And Luke looked a little crestfallen. She giggled. Crestfallen sounded like a "Paige" word. "Vocab at the club," she said, sliding into Parker's open arms.

His body was rigid against hers and he was staring in Luke's direction. "Miller, what are you talking about?"

"Why are you so mad?" she asked, swaying with the walls and the floor. "You're too…too…shiny to be mad."

The scowl dropped from his face, replaced by a blank, stunned look. "Shiny?"

She leaned into him, breathing in the subtle cologne he wore, with his scent underneath. So warm and inviting. She rose up on tiptoe to graze her nose along his collarbone. *Smells so good.* "When did you start wearing cologne?"

His eyes flew open wide. "Were you just…smelling me?"

"Yeah." She twirled under his arm, tripped and fell back against him. "Oops. The floor is whirly."

"I'm shiny, and the floor's whirly." He turned her around, supporting her with an arm around her waist. With his free hand, he tilted her chin up and peered into her eyes. "Have you been drinking, or are you delirious?"

"I'm not drunk." There were two Parkers in front of her. Which one was the real one? Should she kiss him and try to find out? She giggled again. "I'm just glad you're here. Oh! I forgot tell you—*so* sexy with the towel thing in the window. You should do that again sometime."

She rested her head against his chest and hummed along with the music, in time with his heartbeat. His pulse was going really fast, and he'd tensed up some. To make sure he was okay, she snuggled right up against him. *This* was where she belonged. She didn't care who knew. She probably would tomorrow, but she didn't care at the moment. He was warm, solid, and his arms wouldn't let her fall. She could live here, stake a claim, make her home. If only he'd let her.

He turned them in a circle, and his body slowly unwound and relaxed, and his arms closed tighter around her.

Black spots danced in her vision like negative stars. "I like dancing with you."

"Do you now?" he asked in a hoarse whisper. "And why's that?"

"You're my best friend." She took a deep breath of his cologne again. Damn, so sexy. It made her knees buckle, and he tightened his grip. "You make me feel like me."

He paused in their rotation, staring down at her. "You make me feel like me, too. Not Luke's little brother, but myself, separate from his reputation."

"And what a reputation," Zoey slurred. "He's a hussy."

"A hussy?" Parker choked on a laugh. "What's going on with you? You're acting so weird."

"Just a little dizzy spell." She spun in his arms again, but this time, she teetered and he had to lurch to catch her. Her head hurt, and her stomach rolled over. "I want to take a nap. Think I can lie down on the floor?"

"Not this floor. It's nasty." He reached up and put a hand on her forehead. "God, you're burning up."

"I'm too hot to handle." She leaned heavily against him. "I want to go home."

"I think that's a very good idea."

Chapter Twenty-Three

PARKER

Parker moved Zoey off the dance floor. She tripped over her own feet more than once, then tried to lie down on the club's floor again.

"Not here, Miller." He held her up, scanning the crowd for his brother. He had the extra keys for the Jeep, but he wanted Luke's help walking Zoey to the car.

Even more, he needed a little distance before he exploded. He'd gone to get her a drink of water when they made it into the club, and turned around to find her dancing with Luke. He'd been so hurt by that, but turned out he was dead wrong to be. Zoey was all over him, and he'd gone fever hot, too. She'd *smelled* him. What was that about? Was she telling him she was into him? Had her inhibitions dropped with each degree her temperature rose?

"You look good with purple hair," Zoey breathed into his face, leaning in close enough to press her breast into his arm and severely test his self-control.

Where the hell is Luke? "My hair isn't purple, baby."

"Yes it is." She pointed at the purple strobe in the ceiling. Ah, it must be shining down on him. "Did you call me baby?"

"Yep." He led her over to the exit, still searching for his brother. "Like it?"

"Hmm." Her forehead wrinkled. "Nope."

That would've shot a dart of ice straight through his chest if she hadn't sounded so comically sure. "Okay, what *should* I call you?"

"Buttercup, I think." She nodded. "I like that."

"As you wish."

Her eyes lit up. "I love that you love my movies."

There was no way she'd remember this in the morning, so what the hell. "I love everything you love."

She nodded seriously. "Me, too."

He snorted. She really needed to get home before she did or said something she'd hate herself for. Or hate him for witnessing. But Luke wasn't anywhere to be found.

Fine. He'd leave Luke to fend for himself.

P: *Z sick. Taking the Jeep. Will come for you later.*

He bundled Zoey into her coat. "Let's go for a walk."

As soon as they hit the frigid air outside, Zoey started shaking—full on, teeth-chattering, bone-rattling chills.

"C-cold," She blinked slowly, like she could hardly keep her eyes open. "Cold."

"I know you are, Buttercup. Just hold on." He helped her into the Jeep, then ran around to get it started and blast the heater.

She leaned against the headrest, trembling, eyes glassy. He hopped out and pulled the blanket out of Luke's emergency gear. Once she was tucked in with all the heater vents pointed her way, he started for home, pissed that Luke hadn't even answered his text.

"I'm sick," she whispered, still shaking.

"You'll be okay. We're almost home." He pulled his phone out of the center console and pressed it to his ear. "Hey, Brian? I'm on my way there with Zoey. She's sick, and I'm not sure she'll make it to the door on her own. Can you watch for us?"

He didn't ask any questions, merely saying, "Yes. I'm at the door."

"Good. We're turning onto our street now."

Parker drove the Jeep straight into her driveway and came around to help her out the car. She stumbled. "Is it an earthquake?"

He didn't answer. Just scooped her up into his arms. No way she'd make it to the house on her own. Her head lolled against his chest. The front door was flung open and her dad hurried toward them. "Take her to the living room."

Parker set her down on the couch and her mom moved him aside to take off her boots. "I knew she was getting sick. I should've made her stay home."

"Bird flu," Zoey said matter-of-factly, and it almost sounded coherent.

Jen laughed. "It's *not* bird flu, honey."

Parker went to the dads. "Will she be okay?"

"Depends on what it is," Brian said. "But I imagine she'll be fine in a day or two. Good call on bringing her home."

"Yeah, she wasn't making much sense." Although, he hoped she meant some of the things she'd said. "I need to drive back up to the club to pick up Luke. I couldn't find him, and he didn't answer my texts, so I ditched him."

His dad nodded, looking perturbed. "Sounds like he had that coming. See you home in a bit."

Zoey lifted a heavy hand from the couch and waved. "Thanks for…knight…armor."

He gave her a small smile. "As you wish."

"Where did you two go?" Luke was standing on the sidewalk outside the club, looking livid. "I left to look for you, and they wouldn't let me back in. I've been standing out here for twenty minutes."

Served him right. "Didn't you see my text?"

"I left my phone in the car, dumbass."

Oops. Okay, that was on Parker. "Zoey got sick. I took her home. Surely you can't be pissed off about that?"

"There are a great many things I can be pissed off about today." Luke motioned for Parker to get out so he could drive.

Parker didn't budge. "Get in and air your grievances while I drive, asshat."

Someone on the street honked behind them, halting any argument Luke might have made. Grumbling, he yanked the passenger door open and climbed inside.

Parker pulled away from the curb, waving at the impatient driver. "Let's hear it, then."

"It's nothing."

"Oh, so you're going to grump at me that you have things to be pissed about, then clam up when I ask about them?" Parker's hands clamped down on the steering wheel. "Nice, bro."

Luke sighed heavily. "What was going on with you and Zoey? She was all over you earlier."

Uh uh, no way. He wasn't playing this game. "She was all over you, too."

"Not in the same way." Luke pointed at him. "That's why I left. You two didn't look like you needed a third wheel, and you know I don't like to lose, especially twice in one day." He glared out the windshield. "Your turn, what's going on with you and Zoey?

"I'm not sure," Parker said carefully. He didn't know if the bet was over, if he'd won, no matter what Luke thought. He'd probably better keep it quiet. "She was kind of delirious."

"Huh." Luke scratched the back of his head. "She *did* seem a little out of it."

Parker didn't respond. He'd heard some of the things Luke said to her. He'd waited, just off the dance floor, for a chance to butt in. Luke had been pressing pretty hard, and Zoey had dodged all his advances.

But she'd *smelled* Parker, and plastered her body against his. That wasn't something a best friend did, high from fever or not. Had she decided Luke wasn't the right Madison for her? She'd been spending less and less time around Luke the last few days…

The air slowly left his lungs as the reality of what was happening sunk in. If anything that she said tonight was true, even just one thing, then he knew.

Zoey was falling for him.

He let out a soft laugh, and gravity seemed to fall away faster than it did at the apex of a big jump. Best. Day. Ever. Oh, he'd thought that when he won the competition, but if all this was falling into place with Zoey, then it was absolutely true.

"What's wrong with you?" Luke narrowed his eyes. "You look like you've been sucker punched."

"I have been, bro." He turned onto their street, grinning away. "I totally have been."

Chapter Twenty-Four

ZOEY

Quiet voices hummed in the background and the world slowly turned gray. Zoey was lying still on something soft, and it smelled like home, of Dad's cigars and coffee cake. It took a ton of effort to open her eyes, and even then she wanted to shut them again. "Mom?"

A cool hand rested on her forehead. "Right here. I brought you some water."

Then Dad was there, too, helping her sit up on the living room couch. The water tasted so good, but Mom took it away before she was finished. "I want some more."

"You need to take it slow," Mom said. She drew an infrared thermometer across Zoey's forehead. "One-hundred-point-one. Better than the one-oh-three-point-six we saw when you made it home."

Zoey groaned and lay back down. One-oh-three? No wonder she felt so bad. "Time is it?"

"After midnight. Think you can make it up the stairs to

your bed?" Dad asked.

She nodded and, between the three of them, she crept up to her room. The stairs warped under her feet, but not as badly as...wait. What all had happened? She remembered leaving for the club, and she was still in her skirt and black top. Everything else, though, was a blur. Something was nagging at the back of her mind, something Parker had said...but what was it?

Dad left and Mom helped her into pajamas and tucked her into bed like she had when Zoey was little. "Need anything?"

"Some sleep, I think." Her bones had started to ache again, but the world had stopped spinning. "I'm tired."

Mom left, turning out all her lights except the little nightlight in the corner. Zoey snuggled down in bed, letting herself be thoroughly miserable for a minute. She hardly ever got sick, so she might as well give in while she sorted out what happened at the club. She remembered driving there. A guy being a jerk, and Luke chasing him away. The smell of Parker's cologne. Had she *smelled him?* Zoey let out a shocked laugh. She couldn't remember much more than flashes, and all of it was jumbled. Except...wait.

Parker said he loved all the things she did.

A hand flew to her mouth. They'd been flirting. Hadn't they? Oh, boy. She only remembered little flashes, but a lot of it was her, in Parker's arms, saying the most outlandish things. And she *clearly* remembered the hardness of his body, pressed against hers.

Sweet baby Jesus. She'd totally come on to him. There couldn't be any mystery as to how she felt about it, not with the way she'd hung all over him.

And he hadn't run.

Zoey flopped onto her back, wincing when her arms and legs protested. How was she going to handle this? Should she come out and tell him, when she was finally well enough for company? This wasn't the kind of thing you texted to someone, so she'd have to wait until she saw him in person, and make sure he knew it wasn't just the fever talking, but how she really felt.

What if her addled brain hadn't remembered everything right, though? What if he was humoring her and thought she was simply delirious and being silly?

Only one way to find out: she had to ask him.

Her stomach twisted at the thought. Or maybe it was the flu…she wasn't sure, and that was a problem.

She'd think about it tomorrow. She needed to rest and maybe she'd have some answers by then.

The next morning, Mom came up with a tray of toast and orange juice, startling her out of a light doze. "How are you feeling, sweetheart?"

Zoey stretched in bed. Her bones didn't ache, and her head was fine. "I feel pretty good."

Mom took her temperature. "Ninety-eight point eight. Your fever broke. Maybe it was one of those little twenty-four-hour things."

"Does that mean I can go out?" she asked, reaching for the toast. She was starving and it tasted wonderful, even if it was a little burned and had barely any butter on it.

"No way," Mom said. "You'll stay indoors today, young lady. If you're fever free tomorrow morning, you and the boys can have your Christmas Eve morning trip to Snowmass, but for now, you stay inside, resting."

Zoey flopped against her pillows, frustrated. She had things to do and a boy to fall in love with. She hoped. "But I suppose that rule doesn't apply to you and Dad?"

Mom was already in the thermals she wore under her ski

gear. She looked down at her outfit, her mouth twisting into a guilty smile. "We already had plans to go out to Buttermilk with the Madisons today, and since you're better, we decided to go."

"So I'm stuck at home all day." She chugged down the juice, and got an idea. Orange juice: brain food for serious plotting. "Can I have Parker over?"

Mom took the tray, nodding. "Of course. You two could have a movie marathon."

"Okay." She held still, but inside she was dancing. A whole day with the house to herself, and permission to bring Parker over. She probably should feel a little bad for not mentioning that he wasn't quite "just a friend" anymore, but what Mom didn't know wouldn't worry her. "I'll ask him."

As soon as her parents left, Zoey threw back the covers and took a hurried shower. It shouldn't have been hard to decide what to wear, but today was the start of something really different, and that made it difficult. Finally, she decided on skinny jeans and a long-sleeved black T-shirt. That way, if she needed to cool her jets because she had everything all wrong, then it wouldn't look like she'd gone to extra effort.

Finally, with shaking hands, she texted Parker and asked him to come over.

She wasn't sure how long she'd have to wait, so she went downstairs and started making cookie dough. If she'd learned anything from Ben—and his mom—it was that baking could cure just about anything: boredom, a broken heart, frustration, nerves. It kept her hands busy and her mind occupied just enough to keep her from pacing the house.

She'd put the first batch in the oven when the doorbell rang. All her nerves came rushing back as she crossed through the living room to open the door, with a big smile on her face.

Luke stood on her doorstep, leaning against the porch wall in an inviting way.

He gave her a full doze of bedroom eyes, and her smile faded. "Oh, I was expecting...um, hey, what are you doing here?"

He pulled a bouquet of flowers out from behind his back. "Get well offering, and an apology."

"Apology for what?"

He held the flowers out to her. "Why don't you let me in and I'll tell you."

"Oh. Yes, sorry. Come in." She led him into the living room. He sat on the couch and she went into the kitchen to toss the flowers into a vase. When she came back, he patted the cushion next to him, eyebrow raised in invitation.

Frowning, she sat in the chair, not sure what he was up to. "So, why are you apologizing?"

His eyebrow dropped and he rubbed his hands together, his expression disappointed, but contrite. "For not being there when you and Parker needed me. He told me how sick you got last night, and I'm sorry I wasn't there to help."

A memory of dancing with him surfaced from the jumble of last night. Zoey flushed. Did she really curl up against him so tightly? Great. "It's fine."

"It's not fine." He scooted over on the couch, moving closer to her. "I meant what I said last night."

Her stomach swooped. She hated how he still had that effect on her. "Honestly, I don't remember what you said."

His cheeks went pink. "Ah. Okay...I asked you out. For a romantic drive."

"Oh." Was that what he said? And what did she say in answer? "That's nice, but I'm under house arrest until I'm feeling better. Mom's orders."

Some of his swagger returned. "Does that mean you'll consider it for later?"

Damn it. Why was he so interested all of a sudden? It didn't make any difference to how she felt, but it was making her uncomfortable. "I'll have to think it over."

"Fair enough." He stood, smiling down at her. "How about coffee tomorrow? Say, ten? I know we usually take a few runs in the morning at Snowmass, but maybe the two of us could sneak away for an hour?"

Looking up at him, his face arranged in a confident smile, it seemed like he knew she would say yes. Zoey felt herself being worked into a corner. If she said no, he'd probably be pissy with her the rest of the trip, and she didn't want to ruin everyone else's Christmas by shutting him down. "We'll see if I can go out tomorrow."

"You need to get better. Can't miss Christmas Eve dinner at our place." He touched her shoulder. The feel of his fingers sent sparks down her spine…and she was pretty sure they weren't the good kind. "Stay put. I'll show myself out."

As soon as the front door closed behind him, Zoey collapsed against the chair. She'd have to meet him tomorrow, even if she didn't want to. He was her friend, and awkwardness would spread if he wasn't speaking to her. She rested her head in her hands. This trip was supposed to be so simple, and now it was a colossal mess. Unfortunately, she knew it could get worse.

Wait, was something burning? "Oh, shit."

She hopped up from the chair, just as the smoke detector in the kitchen started to shriek.

Chapter Twenty-Five

Parker rolled over with a groan. He'd slept in again, and his body didn't forgive him for it. His knees had taken a beating during the competition and his joints were stiff and aching. He felt like an old man, hobbling to the shower. Another reason to ignore the promoter's card. For some people, the constant pain was worth it, but he didn't want to fall apart way before his time.

The house was empty when he wandered downstairs for breakfast, and his parents' car was gone. Luke's Jeep, though, was still in the driveway.

So, where was he?

Suspicious, Parker munched on a blueberry Pop-Tart and looked for him in the garage, the game room, and Luke's bedroom. His brother wasn't home. Had he gotten a ride up to Snowmass? That didn't make sense. Luke never left the Jeep behind.

Parker picked up his phone to check if anyone had texted,

and someone had. It just wasn't Luke.

Z: *Hey. You up yet?*

Z: *Hellooooo?*

Z: *If you don't fear the plague, want to come over? I want to see you.*

The last line of the text shot through him like an adrenaline shot. She *wanted* to see him? In their entire time as friends, she'd never quite phrased it that way.

He bolted down the stairs, heart on fire. He had no idea what this meant, but his brain was making up a lot of scenarios, all of them better than he should probably expect. He couldn't help it. Did she remember their conversation from last night? He hadn't been able to go to sleep right off. At first, it was stress, worrying about how she was feeling. Later, it was the memory of her breath whispering against his neck when she smelled his cologne. Was this it? Had she decided on him?

He checked his phone again before flinging open the front door. The text was nearly an hour old. If she wanted to see him, he needed to hurry, so she wouldn't think he was ignoring her.

When he ran outside, though, Luke was strolling down Zoey's sidewalk, whistling.

Luke turned and saw him on the driveway. "Hey. I wondered when you'd get up. Want to go up to Snowmass? Zoey's on house arrest."

Parker met him on the lawn in between the houses. The snow was ankle high, and the cold seeped into edge of his jeans. "What were you doing over there?"

Okay, so he meant to ask that casually, but it came out as an accusatory growl. Had Zoey texted Luke, too? Telling him that she *wanted* to see *him*?

Luke shook his head, a smile of disbelief tugging at his mouth. "Kid, does it matter?"

"You know damn well it matters." Parker glared at him. "You're playing some kind of game with Zoey, and with me. I have a right to know what you're up to."

"Fine." Luke crossed his arms. "I gave her flowers to apologize for missing you two last night. Happy?"

No, not in the least. "What about the bet?"

"What about it?" His brother shrugged. "It's on until she makes a decision. She hasn't, far as I can tell." He smirked. "She agreed to have coffee with me tomorrow at ten."

On Christmas Eve? But that was when they all went to the mountain for a morning run. It was tradition…and she was abandoning him? For Luke? Again? "Did she?"

"Yep." Luke gave him a superior look. "Whatever you're doing, it isn't enough. You want to win that girl's heart? *Try harder*, because I'm not letting up until Zoey makes a decision. Now, are you coming to Snowmass with me, or not?"

"Not."

Luke pushed past him and went into the house. Parker stood in the snow, shivering without his coat, not sure what to do next. Part of him wanted to rush over to Zoey's and demand to know what Luke had said to her. The other part wanted to slink back home. Neither option would work. He wasn't beaten. Coffee was just coffee…and she did say she wanted to see him. Not Luke, *him.*

Luke was right—he had to try harder. It was time to let it all go and see where the chips landed. If she chose Luke, he'd have to live with it and be happy for her. He wasn't going to go down without a fight, though. No fucking way.

Nodding, he trudged through the snow and rang her doorbell.

Chapter Twenty-Six

ZOEY

When the doorbell rang again, Zoey took her time answering it. What if it was Luke again? She was still upset with herself for agreeing to coffee when all three of them should be together on Christmas Eve morning.

But when she opened the front door, it was Parker. Her body went limp with relief. "So you decided the plague wasn't too scary?"

"I was exposed to your germs enough last night that coming over now won't matter." He smiled, but the skin around his eyes was tight. Something was bothering him.

She let him into the house, wondering what was going on. "Is everything okay?"

"Sure, why wouldn't it be?" He sniffed the air. "Something burning?"

Her breath hitched at his rough tone. Oh, no. Oh, God, he was upset about last night. By the way she'd acted. She'd misread everything and now he was here to tell her that he just wanted to be friends.

She started hyperventilating a little. The thought of him passing her by made her heart thump in painful beats, hard against her ribs. What was she going to do? "Just cookies. I'll make some more later."

"Okay, but maybe I should ask the same question. Are *you* all right?" Parker frowned, and reached out to brush her hair off her face. "You look like you're about to faint."

"I'm still a little dizzy," she gasped out. Tears stung the backs of her eyes. How could she have been so spectacularly wrong about him? About them?

"Maybe we should sit." He started for the living room, but she stopped him.

"Let's...let's go upstairs. To the game room." It was quieter up there, and if her parents came back for some reason, she didn't want them to walk in on a scene. If there was one. Maybe she could hide the fact her heart was breaking until he left.

On the way upstairs, he asked, "Can I ask you something?"

"Sure." She led him up the stairs and to the game room. "You can ask me anything."

"Anything? Wow, that's some offer." He smiled, but he looked torn—like he wanted to ask, but wasn't sure about the answer.

"Only if you answer a question or two of mine," she said, pulling down the pool rack.

"I will, but are you sure you're up to play?" He eyed the pool table dubiously, like it was going to knock her out. "Maybe we should sit and watch a movie instead."

There was no way she was having this conversation without something to do with her hands and an excuse not to meet his eyes. "I'm fine. Fever's gone, and everything. I'm a little tired, is all."

"Then let's play." He helped her set the balls on the table.

"Who goes first?"

"At pool or the question asking?"

He chewed on his bottom lip. She'd forgotten how cute that gesture was, like he was really thinking it over. Like everything she said should be pondered carefully. And, God help her, that was pretty sexy.

It was really going to hurt when he let her down.

If, girl. If he lets you down. He might not.

Right. She'd hang onto that hope with both hands and see what happened before she broke down crying about her screwed up situation.

"How about this. If you sink more than one ball on your break, you ask first," he said. "And if you don't, I get to ask my question first."

That sounded pretty terrifying, given what she wanted to ask—and what he might want her to answer—but she played it off. "I like this game. Then, any time we don't get at least one ball in on a turn, we have to answer a question," she said, waggling her eyebrows at him, making a show of confidence she didn't have. "Pretty soon I'll know everything about you."

"Hey, I'm better at pool than that." He handed her a cue. "Now break, Miller."

She leaned over the table, gripping the cue hard to keep it from shaking. Focusing on the cue ball, she gave it a hard tap, and the colored balls scattered across the table.

The four ball went into one corner pocket, and the seven wobbled dangerously close to the other, but stopped just short.

"Nooo!" she groaned. "Guess I'm stripes. All right, ask away."

He lined up his shot and asked, "Why Luke? What do you see in him?"

His tone was casual, but she saw how tight his shoulders were. Did he still think there was something between her and

Luke? What had she done to give him that idea?

Obviously she'd done *something*, because it bothered him enough to ask. "What do you mean?"

"Come on, Zoey. I've seen how you look at him." He glared at the carpet. "And I saw him leaving your house earlier. He told me you two were having coffee tomorrow."

A stone settled in her stomach and she wanted to sink to her knees. He'd seen Luke leave? Was that what was bothering him, thinking Luke was over here with her, doing God knows what? "He asked. I'm not sure I actually said yes, but maybe he interpreted it that way."

"You didn't answer the question," he said, leveling a gaze at her.

"His? No."

"Mine," Parker growled.

She shivered. Something dangerous was about to happen, and she'd better be careful. More careful than she'd been last night, anyway. "He's a good friend," she murmured. Squaring her shoulders, she looked Parker in the eye. "That's all."

Parker stood up without shooting. "Funny, it seemed like you had a crush on him."

"I also had a crush on the Channel 5 weatherman when I was eight, certain I'd marry him." She laughed. "Things change."

"In three days?"

She looked away from the weight of his stare. "Yes. Sometimes that quickly."

Parker didn't say anything about her answer. Instead he hit the cue ball so hard it skipped off the table. "Damn it."

He was coiled so tightly…she'd thought his aversion to her spending time with Luke was overprotectiveness. But what if it was something more simple: jealousy?

A little bubble of hope filled her. "My turn!" What could she ask that would steer the questions the right way? It had to be something suggestive, but safe. Something to get him talking, and off-balance, but away from the subject of Luke. Hmmm… "How many girls have you kissed?"

"Seriously?" he said, sounding embarrassed. "Come on."

"Nope, you asked about Luke, you can answer this."

"You really want to know?" he asked, walking slowly her direction.

Not sure what he was planning, she nodded. He kept walking until he stood right in front of her. Close enough that she could feel his body heat, which in turn, made her want to lean toward him, feel his body against hers. Giggling uncomfortably, she backed up instead. He followed until her legs hit the pool table, and stopped just short of touching her. Staring at her mouth in a way that made her think he might just kiss her this time, he said, "Three. Or four if you count the kiss on the cheek you gave me."

"I don't think that kiss counts." Her pulse beat harder than it had during her first black diamond run of the year. His nearness was intoxicating. Best friends didn't make you feel like you were in freefall. And "just" best friends didn't sway your direction like he was a magnet and you were steel.

That was because he wasn't *just* her friend, and they both knew it, even if they couldn't quite say it out loud. She'd been right—something dangerous was definitely happening, and she was ready for it.

"Maybe we should try it for real, though. Kissing, I mean," she murmured, staring at his mouth, wondering what he tasted like. A shiver ran up her spine. "You know, for practice."

He smiled slowly, and his lips were a breath away from hers. She tilted her chin up, waiting for him to make a move, hardly able to stand the suspense.

Instead he backed away, still smiling that mysterious smile. "You might still be contagious."

She stared at him in frustration. Her entire body ached

for him, and he walked away. Was she going to have to draw this out of him, inch by inch? "You're a big tease, Parker Madison."

"Hmm, you think? Now, your turn."

Her hands shook on the pool cue. She reset the cue ball and took a look at the table. The six was at a funky angle to the right middle pocket, but maybe she could make it work. Nothing else was even doable.

Except Parker.

Oh, dear God, that thought popped into her head with far more ease than she would've believed three days ago. Her body felt so hot, she wondered if she was glowing...or running a fever again. This guy was going to drive her crazy. Blowing out a long breath, she took her shot. And missed.

"I'm really starting to hate this game," she said.

"It was your idea." Thankfully, this time he stayed six feet away. "Is there a guy you like?"

You! was on the tip of her tongue. Her more reasonable self clucked its tongue in her head. *You need to slow this down. It could be amazing, but it's early enough to ruin it. Don't fuck this up.*

There were days when she really didn't want to listen to her more reasonable self, but taking things slow wasn't a terrible idea, even if she was one to race ahead of the curve. He hadn't kissed her, after all. Fine, two could play this game. It would be interesting to see who confessed first.

Zoey forced herself to stare at a point over Parker's left shoulder. Her face burned, but she said, "Yes."

"Fair enough," he said softly, and when she looked at him, he turned away, ears pink. He lined up a shot and hit the easy seven into the corner. He took a swipe at the three, but missed. "You're up."

The three had knocked the six into a better spot, and she sank it easily. She got the two as well, but missed the ten. When

Parker went to line up for his shot—a really easy corner for the five—she walked over and blew in his ear right as he was about to strike the cue ball. He'd been distracting *her*. It was only fair that she did the same.

The cue skidded off the table and the cue ball rolled about two inches, then stopped.

"You cheated," he said, pointing his cue at her.

"Is there a girl *you* like?" she asked. The answer terrified and excited her enough to make her knees knock together, but she held his gaze steadily.

His face flushed scarlet. "Yes."

His reaction made her want to ask the big question. "Hmm, I really hope you miss the next one," she said, before sinking the ten. She went after the fourteen next, using it to scatter the solids across the table. Let him avoid her questions now. Ha.

Parker stared her with a look of helpless outrage on his face. She'd effectively ruined just about every shot he had. He went for the three again, and missed. "Damn. Okay, ask away."

She smiled. "Do you want to kiss me?"

Chapter Twenty-Seven

Blood was roaring in Parker's ears. That wasn't what he thought she'd ask, but he didn't mind answering, so long as his actions spoke louder than words. It was time to get real with this thing. She'd obviously blown Luke off, no matter what his brother said, which left him with only one real conclusion. He just needed to confirm it.

He set the pool cue down, and stalked after her. Her eyes went wide and she giggled as she tried to back away again. This time she got around the pool table, but ended up against the wall. He put a hand on either side of her shoulders and swayed dangerously close to her, just enough that her chest brushed against his. She froze, staring up at him with wide eyes.

"Yes." He didn't let his gaze leave hers.

Her expression faded into something hungry, but unsure. "Are you being a tease again?"

"No." He shifted closer so that they were touching—just

barely—and slid his hands down to her hips. God, he wanted to kiss her. Maybe then she'd realize he was the right choice—not just for this, but for everything else in her life, too.

Her gaze lowered, checking him out. When she looked at his face again, her eyes were glassy, and that set him on fire. "Don't leave me hanging, then."

With a wordless growl, he pressed his body tighter against hers and kissed her like his life depended on it. She was the sun, the air. She trembled against him and her arms came around his back, pulling him closer. With one hand tangled in her hair, the other on her hip, he pulled away to kiss her jaw, her neck, her collarbone, tasting her, drowning in her. He would've kept going if he hadn't kissed a salty spot on her cheek.

Zoey was crying.

"What is it?" Alarm beat a hard rhythm in his chest. He took a small step away and let his arms drop to his sides. Had she changed her mind already? "Too much?"

"No, it's not that." She swiped the tears from her face with the back of her hand. "I'm just confused."

Confused? He'd kissed her with everything he had. What was confusing her? "Why, Buttercup?"

She startled and stared at him. "What did you call me?"

A smile tugged its way free from his worry. "Um, you don't remember that, do you?"

She shook her head. "Was that something we talked about last night?"

"Yeah." Unsure how she'd react, he ran his hands up and down her arms, fighting off a grin when her pupils dilated. She liked it when he touched her. "You gave me instructions about pet names."

"You'll have to tell me what happened last night. I'm missing…pieces." She swallowed hard, and he couldn't help watching the movement of her throat. God, he wanted to kiss her again, but she put a hand on his chest, pushing him back. "I'm confused because I need a straight answer. I think we're avoiding saying something important out loud. I know why I am, and it's probably the same for you."

He held very still, and a tiny thrill of fear caught in his chest. "Probably."

"Then say the words, Parker." She put a hand on his cheek. "Tell me why we're doing this."

He pressed his forehead to hers, and a lump grew in his throat. He'd thought about doing this with flowers, or a candlelit dinner, or with some other grand gesture, but here it was, on a random Thursday, in the middle of the afternoon. He sighed softly. "I don't want you to be with Luke. I want you to be with me."

Her arms slid around to the back of his neck and tears filled her eyes again. "Then it's time for me to be honest with you. I did have a thing for Luke. But the more time I spent with him, the more my eyes were opened. I realized what I thought I felt for him was something shallow, just like all those guys at high school feel for me. Like I'm a trophy to be won." Her fingers traced his hairline, making goose bumps rise on his neck. "Then I saw you on your board the other day, with your friends. There isn't anything fake about you. What you see is what you get, and I like that. Something clicked. After the competition yesterday, I was sure. The stupid flu got in the way, though."

"What clicked?" His voice had dropped to a raspy whisper and he closed his eyes to better enjoy the feel of her fingers in his hair.

She paused. "Us."

Such a small word. Two letters, nothing special, but it was a whole world, complete. "Us. So my admission hasn't scared you off, then?"

She laughed, and started crying again, but it was the joyful kind of tears, when girls were overwhelmed and couldn't contain it. "Opposite."

He burst out laughing, because his joy didn't want to be contained, either. "Was that what you meant last night? When you told Luke that PB&J were in the opposite of trouble?"

She pulled back, an embarrassed grimace on her face. "Were you listening to all that?"

He kissed her forehead. "Most of it. Sorry, I eavesdropped, but I had my reasons."

"Uh huh." She shook her head in amusement. "Can you tell me what I said?"

"Maybe later." He cupped her face in his hands. "I have more important things on my mind."

She bit her lip and he felt it in his knees. "Like what?"

He leaned closer, closer, then stopped an inch from her lips. "I have no idea."

"I do." Zoey closed the distance and pressed her lips to his.

He'd been wrong yesterday. *Today* was the best day ever. He kissed her with his heart on his sleeve, and he felt something unwind inside of her, some doubt, or fear, or question. This was right, and her body knew it, as much as his did.

He held her against him, no negative space between them. Her mouth was warm and soft and open. He forgot to breathe—she was his. He still wasn't sure what he'd done or said to change her mind, but that didn't matter. They were together, and that was all he cared about.

"Maybe we should move this to the couch," he said against her lips.

She smiled and leaned away a fraction of an inch. "I'm not that wobbly."

"What makes you think I meant you?"

She giggled and wound her arms around his neck. They

were slowly drawing back together, when the door downstairs slammed shut, and Brian yelled, "Zoey, we're home!"

She pushed him away abruptly. "If they find us up here like this, I don't think my parents will be so chill about you coming over while they're gone. That's not an acceptable option, because I want you over here all the time. Quick— turn on the TV and act normal. Or bored. Bored is good."

All the time? He liked the sound of that.

Footsteps clomped up the stairs. "Zoey?"

"Up here, Dad!" She hurried to plop down next to Parker on the couch. "Park and I are watching TV."

He'd turned the cable box to HGTV, which looked suspicious. He knew Zoey liked it, but he'd never willingly watched *Property Brothers* in his life. Brian was going to see right through this.

"She dragged you up here to watch remodeling shows?" Brian faked a huge yawn. "You're a better man than I am, kid."

I don't know about that. "She's sick. I'm humoring her."

"Good plan." He glanced at the pool table. "Zoey, remember what I said about re-racking when you're done. Don't leave this stuff out, okay?"

Zoey's shoulders were shaking, and she had her arms wrapped around her, struggling not to laugh. "Yes, sir. But what are you doing home already?"

"Visibility was awful at Buttermilk." Brian shrugged. "I think Mom was glad to have an excuse to come home. She felt bad leaving you home."

Zoey's eyes were shining when she glanced at Parker. "It was fine, Dad. Sorry I ruined your day."

"You didn't." He stooped to kiss the top of her head. "I felt bad about leaving you, too. Oh, and Parker? Your mom said you should come home to help get things ready for tomorrow."

"Will do."

As soon as her dad left, Zoey collapsed in a fit of silent giggles. "This is going to take some getting used to, worrying about being busted by the parents."

"It's worth it."

She laid her head in his lap and looked up at him. "I think you're right. But, you know what I have to do next, right?"

He nodded. "You have to have coffee with Luke tomorrow."

She sighed. "Yeah, it's time he moved on to the next girl."

Yes, it was. "Do you want me to go with you? For moral support?" Although that might be awkward, and Luke might think he was there to gloat, which he never would. He was too happy to rub it in.

Zoey sat up and leaned against his arm. "You know what, I should do this myself. It's only fair. Meet me up there after, say eleven? We'll run down a trail or two, then come home."

He rested his cheek against her temple. "Sounds good."

She gave him a quick kiss goodbye and he went home. Mom was already at work on the desserts for tomorrow's dinner, and the house smelled like cinnamon and allspice. Luke called down to him, "What are you smiling about?"

He really wanted to smirk and say, "I spent the last half-hour making out with Zoey," but that was her news to tell. "Next door. I played some pool and watched TV with Miller until her parents came home. She's feeling better."

Luke eyed him from his perch at the banister upstairs. "I hope so. We have a coffee date tomorrow."

"Yeah," Parker muttered, heading to the kitchen to help his mom. "You do."

Chapter Twenty-Eight

Zoey

"'Twas the night before Christmas Eve, and all through the house, not a teenager was stirring, not even a Zoey," Dad sang from the doorway to the kitchen. "Are you feeling ill again sweetheart? You're flushed, and you've been staring out the window for half an hour."

Zoey startled. She hadn't seen him come to the door. She'd been curled up on the living room couch, in front of the fire, staring out at the backyard. They'd had snow since she and Parker made snow angels, and the ground was a pristine white, glowing in the light from the windows from the kitchen. She'd turned out all the lights in the living room, and the fire flickered behind her.

"No, I'm not sick." She gave him a small smile. "Just tired. I want to be rested so I can go up to Snowmass tomorrow with the guys. It's tradition, and I'm not missing it."

She delivered that last bit firmly, and Dad chuckled. "You've been fever-free all day. I don't see why you couldn't go."

He went back into the kitchen, whistling, and she was relieved to be left alone again. Her heart—and mind—had been too full after Parker left for her to be good company for anyone. She'd texted Paige, and her friend had been over the moon, demanding to meet—or at least FaceTime with—Parker so she could see what kind of guy could win Zoey's heart. She decided to take a selfie with him tomorrow at Snowmass, because that was as *them* as she could get, and it would paint the perfect picture for Paige.

The thought filled her with happiness, but that was tangled with what she had to tell Luke. She'd texted him to say she was well enough to meet him, but she was glad Parker would meet her after all the fireworks were over. She didn't want him to be there until she talked to Luke—they were still brothers, and Luke would take it better if Parker wasn't there. Still, she wished that part was already over, because the thought of hurting him made her stomach queasy.

Zoey snorted. That was *her* ego talking—Luke wouldn't be all that hurt, and not for long. His interest in her seemed so temporary, so passing, that she thought he'd play it off and move on to the next girl that afternoon. Still, it might sting a little to hear that his latest conquest was blowing him off for his own brother, the same little brother who'd lived in his shadow their entire lives.

Hopefully Luke would see Parker's sudden breakout as a good thing. *She* did. He deserved every amazing thing that happened, for being patient, good-natured, and kind. Maybe Luke could learn something from that.

Mom came into the living room, leaving Dad with the dishes. He whistled loudly behind her, like he always did when she abandoned him by the dishwasher. Mom laughed, and Zoey's chest ached, seeing what her life could be in twenty-five years. Her parents still loved each other, and enjoyed their own company. What would that be like, being with your best friend for your entire life?

She wanted to find out.

Mom sat next to her and stroked her hair. "It's getting really long."

"I know." She leaned into her mother's hand. "Mom, can I ask you something?"

"Of course, sweetheart."

Zoey stared intently out the window, not wanting to see Mom's expression, in case she was disappointed. "How would you feel if I went to Colorado State, instead of UT?"

Mom's hands paused, then restarted combing through Zoey's hair. "Is that what you want?"

"Yes."

"What made up your mind?"

"A lot of things." Now for the hardest part. Would she be happy? Or freaked out? "But, mostly Parker."

Mom's hands paused again, and the silence stretched out. "How did Parker help you decide?"

She thought about their talk the first day she was in Aspen, when he said they should go to school together, and snowboard all weekend. He'd been trying to tell her what he wanted for them then, but she hadn't been listening. She was now, though.

"Because, he and I…" How did she say this? Talk about awkward. "Um, we're…we've decided to be together. As a couple. I know it's weird, but— "

Mom burst out laughing. "Oh, my God, finally. The tension was killing me, child. *Killing* me."

Zoey's head whipped around. "Uh, what?"

"Tina and I have been waiting for you two to figure it out for more than a year, since summer before last." Mom's eyes were shiny with unshed tears. "I was worried for a while, because I thought you might have a thing for Luke, but I didn't want to interfere and Tina told me it would blow over. Which was good, because Luke's not your type. Parker is. You and Parker are two halves of one whole, and it's high time you realized that."

Zoey stared at her mother, shock zapping at her nerves. "Wait, you and Tina have been *plotting* about the two of us?"

Mom fell back against the couch, laughing. "No—we didn't plot to arrange a marriage or anything. We watched and waited for nature to take its course with you two. Took you a while, though."

Zoey's shoulders relaxed. "Oh. Sorry it took us so long, then. I mean that—if I'd come around sooner, I would've been happier longer."

"What matters is you did come around." Mom kissed the side of her head. "You do realize this means your dad won't like it if Parker's over here when we aren't home."

Zoey dissolved into giggles. "Parker and I had that exact conversation this afternoon."

Mom's eyebrow rose. "And *why* did you happen to have this conversation?"

"No reason." She sat up and smiled innocently. "But, out of curiosity, how do you feel about him coming over when you're not home?"

She braced for a lecture, but Mom just shrugged. "You're eighteen, he's eighteen, and now you're going to college together. If I don't trust you today, how will I ever trust you?" She smiled. "Just don't give your dad a heart attack, though. He's pretty protective of you...which is why I think he'll be glad to see you with Parker."

Dad appeared in the kitchen doorway again. "See who with Parker?"

Mom gave Zoey an encouraging pat on the pack. Right. "Me, Dad. Seeing me with Parker."

He cocked his head, tapping his temple, pretending to

consider it. "Yeah, okay."

Then he went back into the kitchen, leaving her open-mouthed, and Mom smiling. "Like I said, sweetheart, we've been waiting a long time for this."

Funny how the things you're scared to say have a way of working out without damage. She turned to her mom. "I'm glad we have the college thing settled...but I want to explain why it took so long. I have no idea what I want to do for a living, and that made it hard to decide. Now that I know *where* I want to go, any ideas?"

Zoey held her breath, watching her mother's expression go from surprised, to considering. Finally, Mom nodded slowly. "You aren't the type for an indoor desk job. But, honey, you can do whatever you want, as long as it makes you happy, even if it takes a few false starts to get there. Take classes that interest you and see what shakes out. Live the life you want to. That's all I want for you."

Zoey leaned back against the couch, feeling a weight come off her shoulders. Finally, she was figuring out more than her love life. She was figuring out herself. "Good advice."

"It is." Mom rose and patted her leg. "For here, and at home. Maybe it's time to let someone else take on the world at Alderwood."

That sounded familiar—it was the same thing she told Paige in October. She hadn't followed her own advice, but it was time to listen. "I will."

Zoey's left foot bounced under the table as she sipped her latte. Luke was late. Parker had texted to say Luke had left the house and to wish her luck at nine-fifteen. Now it was ten-fifteen. So where was he? Her stomach was churning. There was nothing worse than waiting to deliver bad news.

A ripple of movement ran through the room as the door swung open—all the women turned toward it. Zoey set down her coffee. Only one person had that kind of effect on the female population of a room, and he was probably dazzling them all with a sexy smile.

Hands settled on her shoulders, and Luke leaned in to whisper, "How's my favorite snow bunny?"

Ugh. "Hey." She stared at her hands. "You're late."

"Ran into some traffic." He winked and went to order coffee.

Traffic, uh huh—there was a lipstick stain just under his ear. He'd been close enough for her to see it. He was late to a date because he'd been making out with some other girl. She shook her head…this might be easier than she'd guessed.

Luke brought his coffee over and took the chair across from her. The flirtatious behavior disappeared, and he met her gaze dead on. "I think you have something to tell me."

His tone was perfectly pleasant, but he knew something was up. Time to rip the Band-Aid off. "I wanted to meet you this morning because…I get the impression you think we're sort of a thing."

He blinked, noncommittal. Just like his entire life.

"Okay, fine." His expressionless stare was making her angry. "I wanted to meet you to let you know that I'm not available. I'm with someone else, so please stop flirting with me, and I'll stop confusing things by flirting back."

"You're with someone? That's a surprise." He leaned his elbows on the table, bringing his face closer to hers. "Who's the lucky bastard?"

"It's Parker. I'm with Parker." Zoey traced a finger across the scarred wooden table top. Someone had scratched a heart and illegible initials into it. She and Park should come here and add theirs. "Look, Luke, I didn't mean to hurt you. It's just that—"

"You love my brother." His tone was amused, and a little condescending. "I know."

Her gaze snapped up to meet his. Of all the infuriating… "You do? Then why did you ask me out yesterday?"

He took a sip of coffee, watching her over the rim of his cup. "No offense, Z, but you'd given me the impression you were into me." He set his cup down, wearing a wry smile. "I didn't mean to confuse things. You two have always been an item, and I should've stepped aside sooner. Anyway, I'm glad I gave him that little push."

She sat back in her chair, not sure how she felt about being played, no matter how well it turned out. "What kind of push?"

"He didn't tell you?" His eyes sparkled with laughter, and something meaner. "We had a bet to see who could win you first. I thought I was doing a pretty good job of it, but the kid came out of nowhere for the win. I have to admit, challenging me to the contest was a brilliant move."

"You two *bet* on me? Like I'm some kind of…blue ribbon?" Her hand clenched into a fist under the table. "You made me think you wanted me. Luke, that's an asshole move, even for you."

He sat up straighter, offended. "I *did* want you. I still would if you weren't off the market. And let's not forget— Parker didn't exactly say no to the deal."

Zoey's chest heaved with anger. She couldn't believe it. Did it change anything about how she felt? No…her heart ached to be close to Parker, even now. That didn't mean she shouldn't be totally, thoroughly, utterly fucking pissed off, though. "I doubt that. You just wanted to beat Parker at something. Again."

"That would've been the icing on the cake." He took another sip of coffee, but she didn't miss the bright, angry look in his eyes. "Still, I guess it worked out for you two, huh?"

She sat there, mouth open. She couldn't even…there was nothing she could say to show him where he went wrong. Screw it, then. She was out.

Her chair scraped the floor as she stood. "Didn't either of you think that maybe I knew my own mind? That my heart wasn't some kind of game?"

He gave her as smug smile. "Did you? Because from where I'm sitting, you didn't."

It was a fair question. She knew it now, but last Saturday, she'd been convinced of something else…something that was not only false for her, but for Luke as well. "I figured it out for myself, thank you."

The hurt and frustration deepened in Luke's eyes. "Only because I challenged Parker. You never would've noticed him otherwise."

She shook her head. "I don't think so. See, I drifted toward Parker on my own. He made it easy, sure, but I saw him on his board, being silly with his friends, and it's like he was this whole different person, someone I wanted to spend my time with, my *life* with. The feeling I had went beyond friendship, and I knew it was true. He's perfect for me, in every way. And *I* decided that."

Luke saluted her with his coffee cup. "If you say so."

Gah, he looked so self-satisfied, like her newfound feelings were *all* his doing, and she needed to get away before she threw the dregs of her latte in his face. She turned for the door. Parker wouldn't be here for another thirty minutes, but that was probably a good thing. If he showed up right now, she might start yelling. No, she needed some air. Needed to leave this smug, butt-hurt jackass to stew on his own until he found a new groupie to charm.

"Where are you going?" Luke asked, partly standing as if he was going to run after her.

"Out!"

She left him spluttering behind her, and stomped out of the coffee shop into the blowing snow, slamming the door behind her.

They'd *bet* on her. She could believe it out of Luke, but Parker?

She stalked in a circle, seething. The lifts were running, crowded with people on last minute runs before the holidays. It sounded like a great idea: hitting a trail, with the wind in her hair and no Madison boys to drive her crazy was just what she needed.

She went to the lifts, and growled to herself all the way up the main line, wondering how Parker could be convinced to do something so stupid. Had he thought, even for a minute, not to play into Luke's hands like that?

Or what if it was worse than that? What if Parker didn't really feel for her what she did for him? What if his love only ran skin-deep, like Luke's? She still didn't know what they'd talked about at the club, and maybe she'd misheard what little she did remember.

A sick feeling that had nothing to do with the flu settled in her stomach. Parker hadn't said anything about loving her *before* this trip. What if her playing dress-up for Luke had been what caught his eye?

Did he even love the real her?

Uncertainty and anger pounded in her temples as she climbed off the first lift. To the left, there were blue runs that would land her back at Two Creeks so she could have it out with Parker. To the right, the lifts to The Cirque.

Squaring her shoulders, Zoey turned right.

Chapter Twenty-Nine

PARKER

Luke hadn't bothered to say goodbye before leaving for Snowmass. How would he take the news? Probably not well, but that was his business.

Parker had better things in mind. He pulled his phone out and texted: *I'm on my way up now, Buttercup. I feel the need to kiss you breathless.*

While he waited for her to answer, he ran downstairs to put on his ski gear. "I'm leaving!"

"Where are you going?" Mom called.

"Snowmass. I'm meeting Zoey at eleven."

Mom peeked her head into the mudroom, eyes alight. "I'm pretty sure she's having coffee with Luke. Jen told me she's letting him down easy, because she already has a boyfriend."

Parker couldn't help but smile. Boyfriend—she'd called him her boyfriend. Then again, he hadn't told his family, waiting for Zoey to talk to Luke. Leave it to his mom to find out on her own. "Yeah, about that…sorry you didn't hear it from me, and I'm glad you're happy, but maybe we shouldn't gloat when Luke is having his heart broken."

She snorted. "I heard Luke on the phone this morning, making plans for next week with some girl he met yesterday. Being rejected might sting a little, but he'll never settle down. Zoey deserves someone who will stick with her, thick and thin. That's you, kiddo."

Yeah, it was. "Thanks. We won't be long."

"Take my car. The weather is turning." Mom frowned, and glanced at the window, like she had yesterday. "I don't like how the wind sounds. Tell Luke to come home, too. I think we're in for a serious storm."

Parker glanced out the window. A few clouds sped across the morning sky, but nothing boiled on the horizon. Still, his mom was almost always right about this stuff, having lived in Aspen her entire life. Storms brewed up fast in the mountains this time of year. "Will do."

He hurried down the driveway. The wind was gusting and tree branches whipped in the breeze. Mom *was* right—a storm was brewing. Ski Patrol might even close the lifts before he made it to the resort. For once, he didn't mind. Not being able to hit a trail meant more time curled up by the fire with Zoey at his side.

The drive to Snowmass took longer than he liked. Snow started to fall heavily before he made it out of downtown, and people were fleeing the mountain like Snowzilla was on his way. It appeared he was the only fool trying to get *in* rather than get out.

The parking lot had emptied by the time he made it to the resort, already late for his meetup with Zoey. He'd texted her twice to let her know, and to meet him at the café, but she hadn't answered. He hoped that didn't mean she was still hashing things out with Luke.

Luke's Jeep was in the parking lot, though, and the Millers' Mercedes was, too. He and Zoey must still be here. This could be uncomfortable, but what the hell. He was tired of waiting. He wanted to be with her right this second, and all he could hope is that his brother would understand. If Luke didn't...too damn bad.

He scurried through the cold to Two Creeks, pulling his cap tighter onto his head as he went. The lifts were still running, but the temperature had taken a ten-degree drop since he left the house, and the snow fell steadily. Whoever went up the hill now was either crazy, stupid, or both.

The coffee shop was only half-full. It was usually standing room only at this time of day. He spotted Luke right away, lounging at a table near the back corner of the café. His brother was glaring into space, a mug suspended halfway to his mouth. Parker sighed. Someone was in a foul mood for sure. This wasn't going to be easy. But where was Zoey?

He slipped his phone out—no reply. *Great, I'll have to do this the hard way.*

He went to Luke's table and sat. "Hey."

"Zoey admitted she loves you. Pretty adamant about it, too." Luke shook his head and smiled. "You won, bro. Nice work."

"This wasn't about winning." Parker propped his elbows on the table, casual, as if hearing that Zoey said she loved him didn't want to make him dance inside. "It was about making Miller happy."

"And I think you will."

Parker frowned at him. "Why are you being so cool about this? I thought you'd be a little irritated, at least."

"Oh, I'm not irritated." Luke chuckled in a self-deprecating way. "But it will be interesting to see how she handles seeing you after I told her about the bet."

Parker's blood ran cold. He leaned across the table,

getting in Luke's face. "You *what*?"

"It only seemed fair she should know." Luke shrugged, although Parker could tell he was pissed about losing.

"And I told you she'd walk out on us if she knew." Parker slammed a fist down on the table. The café quieted down and people stared, but he didn't care. "Where is she?"

Luke made a face and Parker braced himself for bad news. "She, uh, she was pretty mad at me after that, and she left."

Parker sat up straight and cocked his head with worry. "Where did she go?"

Luke spread his hands. "How am I supposed to know."

"Surely you saw which direction she went. Her car is still here. Where. Is. Zoey?"

"She said she was going out, that's all."

Oh, Jesus. The car was still here…oh, God, she *didn't*. "Did she take her board when she left?"

"Probably." Luke shrugged. "I wasn't exactly watching."

Parker leapt to his feet. "You complete ass. There's a storm coming in, and she went up alone. You just *had* to tell her about the bet to make yourself feel better, didn't you? And now she's up on the mountain without us."

He went outside, his heart lurching unevenly at the thought of her out there. *Please let her board still be here. Please let her board still be here.* But the rack was empty. Snow swirled, and the wind howled between the buildings. Overhead, dark clouds hung low over the mountain. Zoey was out there, alone, in this.

Luke burst outside behind him. "Where do you think she went?"

"Where do you think?" Parker grabbed Luke's collar and slammed him against the wall of the café, glad to have an outlet for his fear. "She's up on The Cirque. What better place is there when you're completely pissed and need a good run?"

"If that's where you think she is, that's where she is," Luke said quietly. "You know her best."

He let Luke go and ran to the Land Rover. His cheeks were already going numb. He had to find her, make sure she was okay. How much longer would the lifts run? He pulled his board and survival backpack out of the back. If she took a fall up there, all alone, it might be hours before Ski Patrol made the rescue attempt. In this weather, waiting hours would be too long.

He ran to the lifts flat-out, and footsteps padded through the snow after him. Luke caught up and hopped onto the Two Creeks lift with him. "We'll find her."

"We wouldn't have to if it wasn't for you!" Parker turned his back on Luke. "If anything happens to Zoey, I'm going to beat you unconscious."

"And I'd deserve it," Luke muttered behind him.

Chapter Thirty

ZOEY

Zoey skated off the Sheer Bliss lift and made her way over to the surface lift that ran up to The Cirque. Clouds rolled in from behind the mountain, erasing her view of the higher peaks, even though pockets of sun still reached the trail. The wind whipped her hair around her face. When had it gotten so cold?

The lift guide waved her forward. There wasn't another soul up here. "Little lady, the wind's up some, so this trail isn't the best unless you're an advanced rider. You might want to take the scenic route back down, on Rocky Mountain High."

Rocky Mountain High was the blue course leading down from the top of the mountain. It gave less advanced skiers the chance to come up high, without the daredevil ride back down. She'd taken it before, when she was first learning how to snowboard.

She was just about done with guys thinking they could decide her future. Who did he think he was? Was he this condescending to any of the *guys* who came up here? "Thanks, but I'm good. I've ridden Cirque lots of times."

The man shrugged. "Be careful, then."

Zoey gritted her teeth at his fatherly tone. He was only in his mid-twenties, max. "Will do."

The surface lift pulled her up to the Cirque gate. This was it. She was really doing this. Her stomach fluttered as she peeked over the edge. She could do this. She *could*.

Zoey held her arms up to the sky, taking a deep breath of frigid air. She was done letting other people's opinions dictate who she was supposed to be. She wasn't a Barbie doll, or a girl who needed a guy to tell her what she wants. She had two arms, two legs, and a mind of her own.

God, it felt good to realize that.

Zoey threw her head back and yelled, "I'm unstoppable!"

Then she laughed, because it could be true, if she wanted it to be. To hell with Luke. To hell with hiding her real self at school. To hell with people who didn't think she had a brain in her head. She was free, goddamnit, and it was time she started living like it.

She strapped in her boot. The back binding was a little loose, but it would hold. No excuses—she was doing this. She closed her eyes and said a quick prayer to the Snowboarding Gods, then tipped over the edge.

The overcast skies made the path dim, but she let her board show her the way. It pulled her along, a lonely bird taking flight. The snow squeaked under her and she took a hard cut, squealing at the power of owning the entire trail. She could move however she wanted to. Wherever she wanted to. Goodbye frustration. Goodbye doubt. Today she'd be Zoey, snowboarding queen.

She let out another wild yell, laughing when snowflakes filled her mouth. Tree branches swayed in the wind, visible even as she zipped by. The world was so beautiful. So beautiful.

A hard cut here, a swift turn there, zooming between the

trees, then off the trail, just because she could. She flew over moguls, laughing when she caught air. Once, she even made a quick grab. She'd have to show Parker that later—if she decided to speak to him again. Whether or not that happened depended on *why* he'd agreed to Luke's stupid bet.

Snowflakes gusted out of her way as she flung herself down the steep hill about halfway down the course. Her board felt like an extension of her body, a perfect fit, and her hair streamed out behind her as she flew. Was this how Parker felt when he hit a jump? How Luke felt flying down the mountain?

The track twisted, and entered another copse of trees. Zoey checked her speed, and had to bank hard to miss a group of pines. She drifted out onto the main track, sliding farther than she intended. She turned her body, trying to get back to the other side, but a mogul popped out of nowhere. It was sizable, and uneven. She had no time to prepare, so Zoey softened her knees, anticipating the jolt.

She could do this. She wasn't going to fall. Not today.

When she took air, though, the back fastening came loose from her board, leaving it dangling uselessly under her front foot. She flailed with her arms, coming down hard, and her board flew out from under her. Her front boot popped free of its bindings, and she fell back, slamming into the icy snow so hard, her breath whooshed out. Gagging and gasping for air, she tried to get purchase with her hands to stop sliding, but her body had a deal with physics—once in motion, a body stays in motion.

She was moving too fast and, in a cruel trick, the path veered into the trees, sending her careening into the trunk of a giant pine. She slammed into it with her shoulder, and her whole right side blossomed with pain. She cried out, dark spots dancing in her vision, as snow from its branches landed in clumps all over her body. The impact spun her around into another tree, and this time she wasn't as lucky.

Her head clipped an aspen, and the world went black.

Chapter Thirty-One

PARKER

"I'm telling you guys, the lifts are closed," the park official said at the entrance to the Cirque lift. "It's too dangerous up there."

Parker growled in frustration. "I think my girlfriend went up there."

"Pretty blonde, green ski jacket?"

He stepped forward into the man's personal space in his desperation. "So she did go up?"

"Yeah, about forty minutes ago. I told her it wasn't the best idea for less advanced riders, but she seemed determined to do it. About twenty minutes later, we had a call saying to close down." The man looked up at the grey clouds boiling overhead. "I bet we close all the lifts, except those bringing people down, any time now."

Less advanced riders? He said that to her? What an ass. "Look," Parker snapped, "I don't care what's going on with the lifts. I'm going up, even if I have to climb the hill on foot."

"Are you sure she didn't come down already?"

Luke stepped in, putting a hand on Parker's arm. "We've been texting her and she hasn't answered. That's a pretty good indication she's up there, possibly in trouble."

"If that's the case, then Ski Patrol can look for her," the man said stubbornly.

"Tell you what," Luke said, all reasonable. "Why don't I give you a report, so we can have them go look. Okay, Parker?"

He sounded so sensible, but Parker could see the gears turning in his brother's head. He was about to do something reckless.

About damn time.

Parker nodded. "Okay. We'll give a report, but they need to go up right away."

"Do you have a radio?" Luke asked the official.

"In the hut." He pointed to a little building behind the lifts. "Come on, you're welcome to wait inside."

The man started that way, but Luke waited five counts, before whispering, "Get ready!"

He threw the lift switch, and the man yelled, "Hey!"

It was too late, though. Parker grabbed a bar, skating on his board since he didn't have time to buckle his back binding. As he was pulled up, Luke blocked the man from the control panel to give Parker a chance to make it up the hill before the official stopped the lift. Parker knew he'd probably face a wall of pissed Ski Patrol officers when he and Zoey made it down, but he'd take that risk. He'd do anything to make sure she was okay.

The lift pulled him up into the worsening storm. Even though it was barely noon, the sky was leaden gray and visibility was down to nearly nothing. Hopefully, he'd find her standing at the gate, or headed toward the newly running lift.

Knowing Zoey, he'd find her at the bottom, hands on her hips, telling him he was a complete idiot to worry, that she could take care of herself. Either option was fine with him.

He let go of the lift at the top of Cirque. No sign of Zoey. Okay, either she took the lift back down, or she took the trail. Worry made his hands shake as he skated to the edge at the gate. No matter what, he'd run the trail, in case she *was* down there and needed him.

He tightened his bindings as far as they'd go without cutting off circulation, then stood and tipped over the edge. The path was dangerous, covered with fresh powder. He slipped more than once, staying on his board by sheer will. He took the run a little slower than he normally would, so he could stare into every patch of trees. With each turn, he'd slow even more, peering through the blowing snow.

No sign of her. Yeah, she was totally at the bottom of the hill, worrying about *him* now. He had to believe that, or he'd go crazy. He took a sharp turn, jumped an ugly mogul that jarred his teeth, then skidded to a hard stop to rub his eyes.

There, on the side of the hill, was Zoey's snowboard, with the back braces broken and hanging loose. Her hat was a few yards below it, stuck to the ice.

No sign of Zoey.

His knees went weak with terror. Oh, God, where was she? Why was her board here, without her? Was she hurt? Was she…

Stop. Just stop. Think this through, and you'll find her.

Parker forced himself to be still and listen. The wind made whistles and wails in the trees. Snow scrubbed against his cheeks and ice had built up on his eyelashes, but it all came in second to the worry pounding in his chest. He needed a sign, something to tell him where she ended up.

He skated slowly down to her board and picked it up. Six feet away, there was a dent, then a skid mark down the mountain in the snow. It headed into the tree line. She was in the woods.

Parker bent over and unfastened his board. Standing Zoey's board upright, he forced the tail into the snow, then did the same with his, making an X sticking up. The Ski Patrol would recognize that as a distress call.

"Zoey?" he yelled, jogging into the woods. "Zoey? Baby, where are you?"

There, to his right…was that a girl? Or just a drift piled next to a tree? The branches swallowed what little daylight was left, and he could barely make out the marks in the snow. They sailed down into a thick copse. He ran to it—snow had come free from the pine's branches, and the marks had changed course. She must've hit the tree, and spun away.

He turned…and there she was, lying immobile in the snow, limbs flung out awkwardly.

"Zoey!" He raced to her and dropped into the snow at her side.

Terror turned into a live thing, clawing its way into his back. She was so still. He couldn't even tell if she was breathing, and he held his breath, too. There was a cut on her forehead, and blood streaked down her cheek. Her arm hung funny, like it had been broken in her fall.

Praying she was alive, Parker ripped off his gloves and touched them to her neck. He let out a long sigh—there was a pulse and her skin, while cold, wasn't frozen.

Okay, he could deal with this. She was alive, and that's what mattered. She probably had a concussion and at least one broken bone, which meant he shouldn't move her. The temperature was dropping so fast, though, and who knew how long it would take for the Patrol to find them?

Parker stripped off his pack and tore open the pouch that held his survival blanket. The thin foil crinkled and sailed out full in the wind. He struggled to capture it all and wrap Zoey in half of it. "Hope you don't mind a little cuddle," he muttered, shoving his gloves back on and lying down next to her. He tucked the other end of the blanket underneath him to keep it down, then wrapped an arm gingerly around her.

"See? All toasty." He brushed a strand of hair gently out of her face. "Everything is going to be fine. Ski Patrol is coming, and I'm here. I won't let anything happen to you. Okay, Miller? I'm here, and I always will be. I'll do anything for you, even literally freeze my ass off on the side of a mountain in a blizzard."

He said all those things thinking she was out cold, even though he meant them. But she stirred and mumbled. "I'm glad it's you."

"You, who?" he asked, going limp with relief to hear her voice.

"Yoohoo? Who said anything about a drink?" Her words slurred and a little of his panic returned. "Parker. I'm glad it's you."

He pressed his lips to the top of her head. "I'm glad it's me, too."

She chuckled, then moaned. "Collarbone's shot."

"I wondered. How's the pain? Should I go for help?" She didn't answer. "Keep talking, Zoey. Don't go to sleep."

"I'm tired."

"I know." He'd coax her to talk even if he had to babble like an idiot. "Let's play a game."

"Not 'tell the truth.'"

He laughed sadly. "No, I won't suggest that again. How about 'all the things I love about Zoey'?"

"But that makes me sound egotistical, if I talk about me." Her blinks were growing longer, and her body was slowly going slack against his.

"I meant I'd tell you those, and you'd say things like, 'aww, thank you!' or 'really? That's dumb.'"

"'Kay."

"Let's see. Number one: Zoey is my badass best friend."

"I like that one," she said sleepily. "That I'm your friend."

"Uh huh. Number two: Zoey is hot but she doesn't let it go to her head."

A snort…or a snore. He couldn't be sure, so he hurried to add, "Number three: Zoey is kind to her friends."

No answer. He shook her gently. She groaned, but didn't open her eyes. "Number four," he said loudly into her ear. "Zoey is a sleepyhead when she should wake up."

"Number one," she mumbled. "Parker is a dick to tired people."

He laughed in sheer relief. "Yes, yes I am. What else?"

She sighed. "Number two: Parker is a really great guy."

"I try. How about another?"

"Number three: Zoey thinks she loves Parker."

"You do, huh?" he whispered into her hair, wishing he could hold her tighter. This was the first time she said the L-word, and they were stuck on the side of a mountain in a blizzard. The timing sucked, but he'd count it. "I love you, too."

"If I live through this…" She patted his arm with her good hand. Her movements were clumsy. "I'll kiss you for that."

"Then, goddamn it, you better live," Parker said, alarm sending his pulse into a gallop.

"Okay." She shifted a little. "You hear that?"

Parker strained his ears. Shouts of, "Parker? Zoey?" came faintly from the trail. "Yeah. Sit tight. I'll go get the cavalry."

She didn't answer—she'd passed out again. Parker tucked the blanket around her and plowed through the snow, yelling, "Here! She's here!"

Chapter Thirty-Two

ZOEY

Coming back to consciousness was a little like swimming up from the bottom a deep lake. The sun shone up top, a faint glimmer that grew brighter with each stroke, but the trip was a struggle. She hurt all over and sleeping seemed like a much better idea.

"I told you we'd make it back," a soft, warm voice said. A larger hand took hers and squeezed it gently. "And we did."

Zoey forced her eyes open. Parker sat in a chair drawn right up next to her bed. His left hand was bandaged, his hair stuck out in all directions and his eyes were bloodshot and red-rimmed, but his smile was bright…the brightest she'd seen it this trip.

"You were right." She swallowed hard. Her throat was so dry. "My throat hurts."

He nodded, then reached for a cup. "Ice. It'll help."

After he fed her a few chips, her throat felt better. "What happened?"

His smile disappeared and his face flushed. "Luke was an asshole and you stormed out to take The Cirque by yourself."

Oh, yeah. She mostly remembered that part, along with how empowered she'd felt, taking that run alone. Too bad she ended up in the ER. She couldn't make a habit of allowing her girl-power mojo turn into catastrophes. "That was stupid of me."

"Nah. I go on trails by myself when I need to clear my head. Lots of Zen to be had on the mountain. And Luke upset you." His voice was hard, cold. "Which is why my brother has a black eye. See, I promised him that if anything happened to you, I'd beat him senseless. Dad had to pull me off of him in the parking lot when the doctor kicked us out so he could reset your collarbone."

She nodded at his hand. "Is that why you have that bandage?"

"Yeah. I split my knuckles on his jaw."

Zoey winced, which made her head hurt. "I would say you both deserved it, making a bet on me like that."

"Yeah, I know he told you." Parker ran his thumb along her hand, to the inside of her wrist. The room grew warm, or maybe she did. "And I'm sorry. I never should've agreed to something so stupid. If anything, it's my fault you're in here. If I'd listened to my gut and told him no, everything would've worked out."

She nodded. "Probably. But…tell me one thing. Do you really see me as something to be won? Because I thought you knew me better than that. Is all you see the pretty girl, or do you love *me*?"

It was his turn to wince. "I absolutely don't think of you as 'just a pretty girl.' I've never thought about you like that—I know the real you, and the real Zoey is enough for me. I mean that."

She flushed clear down to her toes. "Good."

He breathed out a long sigh. "So…you said something on the mountain. I'm not sure you remember, but I wondered if you meant it."

Now she knew for sure she was warm. "What did I say? Scratch that. What happened after I fell?"

He laughed, and his eyes crinkled in such a nice way. Why hadn't she noticed that before? Sometimes you really didn't see things right under your nose. "Zoey, I—illegally—went up on Cirque by myself in a blizzard to find you. I have the ticket from Ski Patrol to prove it. Do you remember any of that?"

She frowned. She'd hit the tree. Someone had wrapped her in a blanket. She remembered talking, but not what she'd said. "Not exactly."

He murmured something like, "Just my luck," and moved to sit on the edge of her bed. "Okay, so I'll file that entire conversation under Too Long To Explain, and sum it up, how's that?"

The way he was looking at her, like she was the only person in the universe, made her suddenly conscious of the ugly hospital gown and the pull of stitches in her forehead. She tensed up in bed, nervous and a little shy. "Okay."

"I think you said something about, if you lived, you were going to kiss me for telling you I love you. Of course, I said it after you told me you loved me." He smiled and braced his arms on either side of her. "Ring a bell?"

She shook her head, hardly breathing. She told him she loved him? It wasn't untrue…but way to jump on that early, girl.

He leaned closer, enough so she could count the golden-brown flecks in his eyes. "I won't make you repeat it if it was just the concussion talking, but I want you to know I'm all yours, for good, if you'll have me."

She closed her eyes, surprised by the tears sliding down her cheeks. "I'm so sorry. About everything. If I'd just been smarter…if I'd seen…"

"Hey, stop." Parker wiped her tears away with his thumb. "Look at me."

She opened her eyes, and he smiled, something gentle

KENDRA C. HIGHLEY 195

and sweet, all for her. "You aren't stupid. Luke and I were. We never should've dragged you through all this. I should've told you how I felt and let everything work itself out."

She rolled onto her hip, wincing when it jarred her collarbone. "About that L word thing?"

He scooted to the front of his chair and leaned on his elbows so they were eye-to-eye. "Yes?"

She picked at her blanket. After Luke tarnished everything this morning, she felt like she had to be sure, that this wasn't part of his reaction to almost killing herself up on The Cirque. "Did you mean it, or were you scared I was going to die?"

He reached out and traced her cheek with a fingertip. "Miller, we're going to be those old folks telling kids to get off our lawn, remember? I said it because I love you, with everything I am, and have for a long time now. You're my best friend. I love how you act like a kid on Christmas morning. I love how you peel the frosting off your Pop-Tarts before you eat them. I love when you sing—off-key, I might add—in the car without seeming to realize it. There are a hundred little things that make you Zoey, and I love every last one of them."

There were times, like when she watched Parker at the terrain park, that she thought he must be able to defy gravity. Now she was sure of it, because she felt like she was floating, and it was all his doing. He always knew what to say to make her feel like her very best self, like she was worthwhile for being her.

"Are you going to say anything?" he asked, still smiling, but a hint of worry in his voice.

She nodded and crooked her finger to bring him closer. "I owe you a kiss."

He brushed his lips against her cheek. "Just one?"

She tilted her mouth up to his. "Right this minute? Yes. But I think it's safe to assume this is the first of a whole lot more."

Epilogue

Zoey was going to wear a hole in his mom's favorite throw rug any minute. The same one she'd brought home in triumph from an antique show, only for Luke to say the rug looked like a vomit stain. Parker had privately agreed. Maybe he should let Zoey wear it out. His parents were in Cabo with hers, so who would know?

The back of his neck grew warm. Who would know about *anything* they'd done over the weekend? Having both houses all to themselves for the last two days had been…amazing. And they'd pretty much cemented the way he felt about her—Zoey was the air he needed to breathe, to live. She was a part of him, for good.

"Staring," Zoey muttered as she made another round across the rug.

His lips twitched. Busted. "You know I hate that rug, but pacing isn't going to make them get here any faster."

She sighed and crossed the room to drop her forehead against his chest. His arms snaked around her waist of their own accord, almost by memory. It felt good to know he could hold her anytime he wanted, anywhere he wanted, and no one thought it was strange. His heart still did, just a little, and it raced when she leaned into him. The smell of her hair was enough to drive him crazy.

Whatever had he done to become the luckiest bastard on planet Earth?

He pulled her closer. She was here, she was real. Being apart for the last few months had been hard, but that only made this sweeter. Even though he'd memorized the feeling of her body against his, he couldn't get enough of it. He rubbed her back, wishing they had more time. Too bad her friends would be here in five minutes. He wanted to meet them, but time alone with Zoey was too precious to waste.

"Hey, you're okay," he said when she didn't stir. Her body was tense against his, and he needed to fix that. "I don't know what's making you so nervous."

"I'm excited for them to come, but…I kept Aspen to myself for a reason." She tilted her head up to look at him. "What if they don't like it here?"

He reached up to cup her cheek, smiling down at her. "Knowing what I do about Paige and Ben, they're going to love it, because they love you." He cocked his head. "Wait, are you *really* worried they won't like me?"

"There's no way that happens. They're going to love you." She gave him an impish smile. "Because I love you."

"Care to prove it?" He lowered his face close to hers. "I think we still have a little time to ourselves."

Her eyes fell closed as he covered her mouth with his. Knowing that they'd be together for good after graduation made the idea that she'd leave in less than a week more bearable—just a little.

He tangled his hands in her hair. She'd worn it down, and had made some effort with it, which he gently teased her for, before suggesting she didn't need the makeup bag. Her best friend needed to see her face like *he* saw it: real.

A car pulled into the driveway and two doors slammed. Zoey pulled away, her eyes wide. "You ready?"

He pressed his lips to her forehead. With Zoey, he could meet anything head on. "Always."

Acknowledgments

Sometimes books need a little extra love to hammer them into shape. This was one of those books. Thanks to the tireless efforts of the Entangled editing staff, we finally crossed the finish line. An extra serving of gratitude goes to Heather Howland, my senior editor, for helping me plot, plan, and discern where the story really needed to go.

More thanks go to my beta readers, who suffered through a very early draft of this book and gave me the advice I needed to hear. Becca Andre and Kary Rader, you two are the best!

Without my family's support, I wouldn't have time to write at all, let alone herd cats on a draft that stubbornly tried to drift off track. To Tanner and Alex, I love you, and I'm so proud to be your mom. To Ryan, you're the peanut butter to my jelly.

Finally, thanks to you, the readers, for your support over the course of this series. You rock!

About the Author

Kendra C. Highley lives in north Texas with her husband and two children. She also serves as staff to four self-important and high-powered cats. This, according to the cats, is her most critical job. She believes in everyday magic, extraordinary love stories, and the restorative powers of dark chocolate.

Discover more of Entangled Teen Crush's books...

RESISTING THE REBEL
a novel by Lisa Brown Roberts

When loner Caleb Torrs sees spirit committee leader Mandy Pennington pining over some los-er at a party, he thinks she's lost her mind. Maybe he has, too, because he just asked her to be his fake girlfriend. She'll get that guy's attention, and he'll get his stalker ex off his back. Too bad their plan is working, and the loser she wanted is finally noticing the one girl Caleb just might be falling for...

THE SECRET LIFE OF A DREAM GIRL
a *Creative HeArts* novel by Tracy Deebs

Dahlia Greene—aka international pop superstar Cherry—is undercover as a normal high school student. Playing a little matchmaker for Keegan Matthews seems like the perfect opportunity to live a real life. What she doesn't know is that the girl Keegan's been secretly crushing on is her. Keegan figures he'll play along with Dahlia's plan to help him woo someone else, then make his move. But with so many secrets, their romance is doomed from the start...

CPSIA information can be obtained
at www.ICGtesting.com
Printed in the USA
FSOW01n0202140717
36385FS

9 781682 812532